Raunchy Sex Stories

First Time, BDSM, Threesomes, Bisexual, Milfs, Anal Sex, Gangbang, Lesbian and Much More

Michael Renfroe

Table of Contents

Some New Friends

My wife Mary and I met some new friends last Friday evening in a café in the city central when things took an interesting turn.

To describe Mary first, she has 5'6 long, taut legs, big 40D breasts that have just begun to yield to gravity, a round, firm ass and only a hint of a belly. She has long dark brown hair and beautiful deep brown eyes that give a hint of Indian descent. I am 1.90 m tall, have a shaved head to hide the quick baldness, broad shoulders, a somewhat thick belly, but overall a stature that is above average for a man.

We had been talking online with Ken and Kathy for a few weeks, we had met in a swinger's group and talked about movies and general nerdy stuff. This was to be our first meeting face to face, and a café seemed ideal. It is a neutral territory. Nobody feels pressured when they are near a private room, nobody is forced by alcohol to make decisions they might regret later.

When Ken and Kathy came in, I was devastated. We had of course exchanged pictures, even some naughty ones, but the camera didn't do them justice. Ken looked like a male model, like the hero on action figure packages. He was bald, full lips, dark eyes and a natural smile. His shirt bulged and rippled when he moved his arms, his muscles contracted and threatened to burst at any moment. Kathy looked like an Amazon. She was six feet tall, slim, dark night-black, with cheeky breasts, wide hips and long legs, accentuated by a miniskirt that constantly revealed her amazing ass.

I stood up and shook Ken's hand as they approached and gave Kathy a light one-armed hug. We talked for a moment, and then Ken and I went to the counter to order while the wives got to know each other a little. What attracted us to each other at first were movies, and it wasn't long before Ken and I talked at length about the new movies that were coming out, and what movies we thought were hot garbage, and which ones looked so bad they were good. While we waited for our drinks, I took a look back at the table and looked up Kathy's skirt for a moment, not sure if it was on purpose or not. I told Ken that Kathy looked amazing and he replied that Mary was an absolute knockout, an opinion I agreed with, but it was nice to hear others say that.

After a few hours of sitting and talking and three cups of coffee later, we decided to move this conversation to my and Kathy's house to play some board games and get to know each other over drinks.

As we both had a drink at the dining table, we started handing out cards for a few rounds of Cards against Humanity. It was a great icebreaker game full of inappropriate laughter. I kept staring at Kathy and noticed that Ken and Mary were also appreciating each other. After a few drinks and a few rounds we started to play a strip version. Whose card was chosen as the winner was allowed to choose one of the other players to remove an item of clothing. It didn't take long before we had Mary and Kathy stripped down to their bras and panties. Mary was wearing a matching black lace bra with lace-trimmed boys' panties, and Kathie was wearing a red bra and matching thong. Ken and I had both been stripped down to our boxers.

Mary won the round, and as she looked around the table, she finally said: "I just have to see what Kathy's nice tits look like to make the top girl burst! That made us all laugh as Kathy pulled up her bra and let her breasts out. They were smaller than Mary's and perkier, with dark nipple areas on her midnight skin and big nipples. Ken's victory made Mary lose her bra next, Kathy reached behind Mary and unzipped the bra that Mary threw over her head onto the pile of discarded clothes behind her. Her breasts sagged a little, but her fullness and voluptuous nipples still held her full attention.

Kathy won the next round and Mary lost her panties. My wife got up from her seat and stepped onto the table, taking care not to disturb the cards or the drinks, and slowly rolled her panties down her legs, spinning in a slow circle as she bent down and pushed it up to her ankles, she bent down lower and exposed both Ken and Kathy's ass and pussy, she turned her head over her shoulder to Kathy, "is this what you wanted to see?

"Is this what you wanted to see?" "You're damn right it is! The pussy's wet enough to lick stamps!" Kathy replied. Mary stood up and stepped out of her panties and left it in the middle of the table before stepping back. Kathy helped her down and ran her hand up Mary's inner thigh as she stepped back.

"Well, I guess I'm out of the game now, so I get to watch," Mary said as she sat down on the chair with her legs slightly spread.

This time I won, and I looked between the two new friends we'd made: "I can't wait to see Kathy's delicious pussy, but I think if Ken stays in these boxers any longer, his boner will come out of them and tear them apart, so let Ken see what you've got! This surprised everyone a little bit, but only for a moment before Ken started giggling and stood up and peeled off his boxer shorts and revealed a massive cock that was as coconut brown as the rest of him. It hung long and the stuff between his legs was a light ten inches and a good three inches in diameter. It was the second largest tail I had ever seen, and the largest was a soccer player we all hated to shower with in high school because there was simply no comparison. Ken pushed back his chair and occasionally stroked his cock to get it to full erection while Kathy and I finished the last round.

We decided that the only fair way to do this was to give Mary the opportunity to choose the winning card. This time it was Kathy who climbed onto the table and unfastened the strings on the side of her thong that was holding her, as she climbed back down, Mary stood up and grabbed it. Kathy sat down on the table and Mary kissed her. I could see their tongues flirting into and out of each other's mouths.

Mary broke the kiss and lightly pressed on Kathy's shoulder to signal that she should sit back, which she did. Mary then began to kiss her breasts and licked the left nipple first, then the right. She moved her kisses onto Kathy's flat stomach and onto her hips. Mary kissed and then bit slightly on the skin of Kathy's inner thigh. Kathy arched her hips slightly upwards and Mary moved her mouth closer to

Kathy's pussy lips. She teasingly licked her clitoris with the tip of her tongue. As I watched my wife lick Kathy's cunt, I pushed my boxers down and freed my hardened cock.

My cock is thicker than average, but only slightly, depending on my horniness and the weather it is between 6 and 8 centimeter's, it is quite thick, but the best part of my cock is the head. It has the circumference of a tennis ball, most of the women I have been with have no problem taking my full length, but my full circumference is another story. Mary herself had trouble with it until after our second child. Now I watched her sucking and licking this other woman's sweet-smelling pussy and I started to caress myself lightly.

Kathy moaned and pulled Mary's face deeper into her spread legs and lifted her hips as she orgasmed, only to finally calm down again. Mary sat up and then climbed over Kathy's body onto the table, curled up and kissed a new way up her body until she reached her face, kissing her deeply and passionately before turning around and lowering her own soaking wet cunt onto Kathy's eager mouth before diving back hungrily for more of Kathy's sperm. Kathy pushed her tongue inside my wife, licked the outer folds of her lips and then sucked on her clitoris.

As I rubbed my hard cock, I felt a hand gently caress my balls. I looked down and saw Ken massaging my balls, he looked at me and smiled, now I have never been with another man, I have never found any man sexually attractive. I've seen guys that look good, but they didn't do anything for me, but that was sending a little bit of electricity through my loins, that became a full power plant when Ken bent down and started sucking just the head of my cock. He licked and sucked the head and let it jump out of his mouth with an audible pop every now and then. I leaned back the head and closed my eyes as he teased my cock. I had never kissed another man before, let alone had a duck on my cock, it was a strange feeling. I felt the stubble of his bread rubbing against my balls and thighs and tickling as he maneuvered my cock around in his mouth. He was talented at it, he kept bringing me to the brink of orgasm and then pulling me back again.

Kathy and Mary both orgasm together on the table, and Ken kept bringing me to the brink of orgasm before pulling back and letting me calm down. As the women came towards us, Ken stood up and kissed Mary on the mouth while Kathy fell on my lap and wrapped her arms and legs around me.

My cock found her dripping wet appearance easy and she started rocking her hips and pushing me deeper inside. Her pussy snuggled around my cock and stroked my length from the inside. I bent down and licked her nipple, took one in my mouth and bit her slightly. "Mmmmm", she moaned "harder!" I bit harder on her nipple and rolled it between my teeth. She bucked and pressed hard on my lap and I felt her sperm roll past my balls.

Over Kathy's shoulder I could see Mary bending over the table and Ken ramming his cock into her. She gasped for breath and moaned violently as he hammered into her, her hands gripping the sides of the table. She opened her eyes and watched as Kathy twitched in my lap before another orgasm. I grabbed Kathy's shoulders and began to push her body down while I pushed my hips up and penetrated deeper into her until I finally cramped my cock in her pussy and filled her with my sperm. Kathy moaned as I shot my load into her, then she leaned in and gasped for air, kissed me on the lips and then on the neck. She rose from me, small drops of our cum dripping freely and she made her way back to the table and climbed to the top in front of Mary. She spread her legs and pulled Mary's face into her neatly trimmed pussy. "Fuck you clean!" She moaned, "Lick your husband's sperm off my pussy."

That was all Mary needed when she drove her face in and wrapped an arm around Kathy's leg to hold her down. Ken grabbed Mary's hips and punched harder, obviously turned on by the show that was going on in front of him, until finally I saw his leg start to twitch and he cried out a deep throaty moan, and I knew he had just reached orgasm and was emptying his balls into my wife. Mary collapsed on top of Kathy, and Ken staggered back into the chair next to me. This was the first time the four of us played together, but I hoped it wouldn't be the last.

Two Beautiful College Students

Atticus leaned forward and smiled at the sight of the two beautiful young college students that entered his bedroom. The two young women, Holly and Bailey, approached him dressed in sexy, sultry lingerie and pantyhose. Atticus watched them both approach with sensual swagger as he slowly stood up from his chair. "Two little doves, beautiful as can be," he said as his eyes gazed upon their slender, perfect bodies. "Two little doves, belonging all to me."

Both women smiled as they pressed their hands against his fancy black suit. Atticus breathed out and rubbed through their hair. He loved seeing the two girls wearing the clothes he purchased especially for them. Their touch was arousing all on its own. He bit his lip and turned to the table he was sitting at. On it sat two pairs of fancy, pink handcuffs designed to cushion the wrists of the wearer.

 "Put those on each other, my dears," he said as he stepped back watched them eye the toys.

Holly smirked at Bailey as she grabbed both of the handcuffs. She handed Bailey a pair then held out her wrists. "You do one arm then I'll do yours," she said with a sly smirk. Bailey nodded as she took the cuffs and wrapped them around Holly's wrist gently. Holly pulled Bailey into her as she kissed her lightly on the lips. Their breasts rubbed against each other as Bailey returned Holly's kiss while she strapped on the cuffs properly. Holly then cuffed Bailey's wrists as they pressed their bodies against each other in a hot and heavy grind.

Atticus chuckled as he stepped between the two. Without a word, he caressed both their necks and chins as they raised their arms up in the air. Atticus reached up and pulled down the hooks fastened to the ceiling. He attached the hooks to both girls' cuffs as he tightened the chain. Their beautiful bodies partially suspended on their toes. Atticus rubbed his arms down Bailey's back as he snuck his hand down her pantyhose. He looked her deep in the eyes before he kissed on her neck and slowly moved down her body, pulling off her panties and pantyhose.

Bailey shook with a subtle twitch of delight as Atticus kissed her right below her navel. He stood back up and gently popped her breasts out of her bra, discarding the clothes on the floor. Holly stared Bailey down and bit her lip in excitement.

Atticus then turned to Holly and rubbed his finger against her lips. Holly opened her mouth and sucked on Atticus's finger. He smiled as he reached his other hand around and undid her bra. Holly's bare nipples were erect and ready as Atticus pulled his finger from her mouth and rubbed the saliva over her breasts. Holly shivered with excitement as Atticus grabbed her panties and pantyhose and pulled them down to her feet. He balled up the undergarments and tossed them aside standing slowly between the two women. Both Bailey and Holly pushed their bodies against his, grinding their thighs against his fully erect package.

"There we go, nice and easy," said Atticus as he pushed forward gently rubbing his groin against Holly's first. "Good girl," he exhaled lightly as he leaned forward, gently kissing her neck. A moan escaped Holly's lips as she trembled. Bailey looked on in surprise, eagerly awaiting her turn. Both girls shivered in the draft of the cool air as they watched Atticus enjoy them one by one. Next Atticus found Bailey with his strong hands and gently caressed down her back. "Are you just as sweet?" He asked as he leaned forward, grabbing a handful of her hair into his hand and pulling her forward as his tongue met the nape of her neck and licked al the way up into the base of her chin. Bailey too moaned as her legs quaked.

Atticus smirked at them, chuckling lightly as he took a knee. He leaned downwards as he slowly parted Bailey's legs and bestowed a soft kiss to her groin. Her lips trembled as she looked down at him, already moaning lightly in anticipation. The moment his tongue met her clitoris the heat of pleasure rose inside of her. She writhed lightly in the bondage as Atticus' tongue found its way over her clitoris, rubbing it back and forth. Holly watched on, biting her lips in hopeful anticipation. Bailey's moans filled the air as she felt her pussy swell with immense pleasure and intensity. Atticus smirked up at her noting her shivering as his tongue thrust its way inside of her.

After Bailey's pussy was nice, wet, and swollen with pleasure, he moved along the floor back over to Holly who had been watching on in nervous anticipation. Atticus wasted no time bestowing his tongue down on her as well. He parted her legs and lips with ease as his tongue met her pussy lips and he could already taste her sweet cum. She had already grown wet with excitement as she watched Atticus tasting Bailey' and filling her with his tongue. Atticus groaned lightly as he held on to Holly's well-defined hips, kissing up and down the length of her inner thighs before extending his neck upwards to lick again.

"So sweet," he as he nipped at her lightly. She jumped back in surprise and with a gasp as his tongue flicked over her slit. "You're dripping with pleasure my dear," he said as he rose to stand, looking at the two beautiful girls. He smirked at Holly as he leaned forward wrapping his hand around her neck and squeezing lightly. "There is more still to come." He exhaled sharply as he reached downward, undoing the belt from his pants. He made several of his rounds behind the two girls as he took his belt and lightly hit each of them on the ass several times with the tail end of the belt without the buckle. Both girls jumped and squealed in surprise as they twisted in their confines. Atticus couldn't help but feel delighted at watching them squirm. After a few good hits each, he threw the belt to the side and made his way up behind Holly. "You're so wet, I think I'll start with you."

"Yes master," moaned Holly as she bit her lip, her ass still stinging lightly from the spanking. All she could do was listen as she heard Atticus take his place behind her and start to undress. The moment his hands found their way back to her waist she trembled again. This time however she felt his hard cock push its way through her thighs. She bit her lip and swallowed hard as she felt Atticus grasp to her and pump himself between her legs letting his cock slide back and forth over her already pleasured clit. Her toe curled where she stood as she arched her back. The moment she finally found herself able to take a breath Atticus was already pushing himself inside her. Her entire body tensed up heavily as his cock pushed its way over her g spot and up towards her cervix.

Bailey watched on now, breathing heavily as she watched Atticus explore her friend. His thrusts were long and slow at first. Holly could feel every movement of his shaft inside her as it slid in and out. He continued to pump lightly, in and out, in and out, as he stood behind her. He let his hands find their way back up to Holly's neck as he thrusted. He took them both and wrapped them firmly around Holly's neck as he thrust forcing the air out of her and using the light chokehold against her neck to push her back onto his cock with every slow and deliberate thrust.

After a moment of thrusting, Atticus pulled his cock from Holly and began to make his way to Bailey. Holly sighed a little in a disappointment, wishing that he had fucked her longer. Bailey, however, spread her legs willingly the moment he took his place behind her. "Aren't you a good sport," he said as he leaned forward groping her breasts from behind and biting lightly at her shoulder. Bailey twitched lightly as she arched her back where she stood and extended her ass backward. Atticus raised his brow in surprise and delight as he pushed himself deep inside her. "You want it bad my dear?" he asked as he suddenly jerked her backward thrusting his cock deep and hard into her. Holly reeled back surprised as Bailey squealed in delight. Atticus held tight to her and began to thrust faster in response to her enthusiasm. Now each thrust was short, sharp, and deep as he fucked her. He pushed his hips forward with all his might sending shockwaves of pleasure through Bailey's entire body causing her moans to turn to screams and the light quivers of her body to form into rolling waves.

Atticus looked at Holly moaning and wanting more. He took his hand and reached around her ass and down her crack. He pushed his finger inside her and proceeded to thrust them in and out of her with ease. Holly and Bailey both moaned as he simultaneously fucked them both with vigorous passion. He could feel both girls shake as they came hard on his hand and dick. He reached up and pulled the hook on the ceiling, dropping both girls to their knees. He then grabbed Holly and forced his dick down her throat. Holly gagged and moaned on his cock in surprise. Bailey pushed her way up to Atticus' shaft and licked it as it went in and out of Holly's mouth. Atticus moaned as he pulled his dick from Holly and pushed it into Bailey's mouth, force fucking into her throat with more intensity. Bailey gagged and moaned as she could feel his hot liquid start spraying into the back of her mouth. Atticus held both of the women by their hair as he thrusted a few more times, cumming into Bailey's mouth before pulling out and rubbing it over her lips as Holly kissed his head. They two girls then kissed each other to share the semen as Atticus stepped back and breathed out.

"Beautiful little doves, indeed."

A Wild Party

The doorbell of the cafe rang every time it was opened. And every time my heart pounded in anticipation. Two weeks ago, I walked into the cafe for the first time. I sat down at a table, far in a corner, diagonally behind the short side of the bar. I had eaten and drank something and would just go home when I noticed her long dark curls. She sat at the bar with a bunch of girls and was busy talking. Occasionally she turned so that I could see her face in the soft glow of the bar lighting. She was beautiful, very beautiful, but beyond her outer beauty, it was her attitude that appealed to me the most. She moved almost gracefully. Looked at everyone she spoke to, did not smile as loudly as the others, but kept the smile on her lips. She was a friend in the cafe that quickly became clear. Many who came in greeted her kindly with a pat on the shoulder or a quick kiss on the cheek. Occasionally there was someone who was privileged with a kiss on their lips, but in the two weeks I admired her from my quiet corner, there had only been one person where the kiss lasted longer than just a quick greeting kiss.

She was blonde, tall and slender. I had seen her for the first time yesterday. When she came in, the otherwise silent cafe turned into a wild party. She went to the stereo and turned the volume up a little, then pushed some tables and chairs aside and went to the woman with the long dark hair. She pulled her along on the small dance floor and although many of them followed, they continued to dance aside, so I did not lose sight of them. The music was romantic and compelling, the dance slow and intimate. Their bodies are swinging closer to each other to the rhythm of the music.

Their hands touched each other and the fingers intertwined — belly against the back, back against the back, belly against the belly. My heart rattled and my blood burst through my veins. Jealousy became a big bud in my throat that I couldn't swallow. I reached for my glass while not looking away and brought it to my mouth. Forgetting the cool moisture on my lips, I stared in disbelief at what happened before me. The dark woman's face had disappeared behind the blonde hair of her dance partner. They no longer danced, slowly turned away from the group in my direction. I have turned until I saw them kiss. I choked beer and squeezed it against my hand.

The kiss was broken, the woman with the dark hair looked me straight in the eyes and I felt a warm blush spread over my cheeks. The dance was over and she returned to her seat at the bar, but when she sat down, she turned so that she could see me. The blonde followed her and ordered a beer. She tried to start a conversation with her, but the dark woman only nodded occasionally while she kept looking at me. My glass had been empty for a long time and I was still sitting there, enchanted by her look as if she had nailed me in my chair. The blonde stood up and approached me. I was shocked — fiercely. I was not out to make or search for difficulty. Her face was threatening as she bent over my table. "Sarah is mine." Then she was gone.

The doorbell rang when she opened it and left the cafe. Sarah. Her name is Sarah. She has long, dark curls and enchanting eyes. I did not know more, but I could not walk past the door of the cafe, I had walked in like the last two weeks, every day after work. I sat down on 'my' chair with a glass of beer and waited anxiously for Sarah's arrival. The doorbell rang again and I looked up. Sarah came in. She went to the bar on the other side and I could hardly hide my disappointment. She understood me, that's why she sat down somewhere else. I drank my beer quickly and felt in my pocket for some change.

"Hello, can I?" Sarah stood in front of me and pointed to the empty chair on the other side of the table. I nodded because the words were stuck in my throat. She sat down and looked at me in silence, just like yesterday. Her eyes unfathomable, enchanting and my heart missed a few beats. Why was this woman so upset about me? Her warm hand closed around my shaking fingers. "Do you want to talk somewhere else?" she asked. Of course I wanted that. For two weeks I wish I had the courage to talk to her. But the blonde woman's face and her threatening words made me hesitate. "The blonde..." I could hardly pronounce the words, "from yesterday..." The well-known sweet smile appeared again on her lips. "My ex." I sighed with relief. I believed her unconditionally, why shouldn't I?

She came to me. We got up from the table and left the cafe. She walked right next to me and I felt her fingers search. When I looked at her, she smiled shyly, questioningly and I spread my fingers against hers until they were entwined. Her apartment had the same warmth that she radiated. Warmth and tranquility that I had been looking for so long. It was like living in a dream, but the hot coffee she offered me was reality. She sat down next to me on the couch and pulled her feet under her. Her knee is resting on my thigh, familiar as if it had always been like that. We drank the coffee in silence and the cups became cold in our hands without a word falling between us. Her eyes were dark, her hand warm and soft when she put it against my cheek. 'May I?' she whispered. I didn't know what she wanted, but I agreed and nodded. She then slowly leaned toward me and stroked my mouth with her lips. I shivered with excitement, but at the same time, I caught my breath deeply. She wasn't particularly shy. Her warm breath stroked and soothed my trembling lips. I felt the tip of her tongue follow the lines of my mouth. I didn't know if I could do it. I had often dreamed of it for the last two weeks, but I had never kissed a woman before, not like that.

She kept on going, softly, quietly, without rushing or forcing me. My lips opened automatically and let her in. The taste of coffee was still on her tongue. Playfully, expectantly, she kissed me with only the tip of her tongue in my mouth, until I started kissing her back when she came deeper, more penetrating, and passionate. I needed air and broke the kiss. "You've never done this before..." It was not a question but a statement. I looked at her blushing and shook my head. I had never had sex with a woman before. I have seen countless videos and I knew what and how they did it, but it had always stayed that way for me. I was not someone who went out to meet girls and certainly not someone for one-night stands.

Moreover, I knew that many girls were afraid of getting along with me. Afraid that I would find out more than they wanted to tell me. It is not easy to be a psychologist and leave your work at the office. People interest me, what they do and what drives them is always a journey of discovery for me.

'Are you afraid?' she asked as she flattered herself against me. "No," I could admit. I was not afraid because the first time would be with her, with a woman whom I dreamed for two weeks, who filled my mind when I lay in bed stroking myself in the evening until I finally fell asleep tired of many orgasms. "Careful?" I started to laugh. It was a strange way to put me at ease, but she managed it. She also laughed and raised herself from my shoulder so that she could look straight at me. "To be honest, it all just comes over me..." She came and sat on my lap with her knees on either side of my hips and her hands against the cushions of the couch behind my head. "Robbed?" she laughed, "You were the one who sat staring at me in the cafe for two weeks. Do you know what that feels like?" I blushed shyly. So she had understood me much longer. She came closer and closer with her face and I saw her eyes on my mouth. Even before I finally felt her lips again, I had already opened my mouth and let my tongue slowly and softly enter her.

Her fingers entwined in the short hair of my neck and held my head so that I could not break the kiss again. I didn't want it either. I closed my arms around her back and pulled her against me while I lay down on the couch sideways. She was stretched out on top of me, her one leg familiarly pushed between my legs. I felt her move slowly, rhythmically, as if we were dancing and lifted my leg that lay between her legs until I felt it press against her crotch. She moaned and a warm feeling of love and tenderness engulfed me. I longed for her like never before. I wanted to feel, caress and caress her as I had often done in my dreams. As if she could read my mind, she whispered to my lips: "Shall we go to my bedroom?" I moaned my answer. She got up, took my hand and led me to her bedroom where we fell to bed without further words and continued the kiss as if we hadn't moved a step. She was lying next to me now and I missed her proximity. It felt almost bare and empty without her body pressed so tightly against me. But I was surprised by her caressing hands that opened the buttons of my blouse.

She stroked my breasts through my bra. Calm, seductive and I felt the nipples almost painfully hard. My hand slipped under her t-shirt and reached the closure of her bra. Without dwelling on what I wanted to do or how I loosened it and brought my hand to her belly until a warm chest filled my hand. Her nipples were hard and pressed into the soft flesh of my palm. I shut all thoughts out of my mind and left the desire! And take over.

In one movement, I took off her shirt and bra and stared at her well-shaped breasts. She used the opportunity to help me out of my clothes and, without pardon, took off my jeans too, after which she pushed her own pants off her hips and dropped them over the ankles off the bed. She turned back to where I was waiting in suspense. This time her tongue was compelling, her hands fiery and I felt my panties getting wet. Her hand ran down my stomach and grabbed my crotch tightly. I moaned and jerked my hips against the pressure of her hand. I burned with a desire to feel her in me and furiously penetrated her mouth with my tongue. She understood because she pulled my panties off my hips and spread my wet lips looking for my love channel and clit. She found both. Her middle finger slid deep into my wet cunt without difficulty while her thumb gently stroked my clit. I started to move wildly against her finger, forgetting the kiss. I gasped when I felt the first orgasm coming and moaned loudly as it washed over me. I lay silent after enjoying my first orgasm while Sarah slowly moved her finger in and out of my pussy. It was great to have sex with a woman. Even more delicious than I could have imagined. When I opened my eyes again, she was looking at me with a smile of satisfaction on her face.

"Do you know how hot you are when you cum?" she smiled and I blushed at the thought that she had been watching me all the time while I let myself go. Still, it excited me too and I wanted nothing more than to look at her while I showed her the favor.

Rough College Gangbang

When Laura agrees to tutor one of the star football players, she figures she is in for a dull night but needs the double-payment. What she never expected was to find herself tutoring several members of the offensive line, including a thorough oral exam.

I was not one of those girls who was in college for the parties and the husband. I really wasn't. At least, I did not start out that way. I was a good girl in high school and even started college the same way. My first three years, I maintained an A average and was in all of the honors classes available. I am almost certain that the other students made fun of me for sitting in the front and asking all kinds of questions, but I did not really care. I know I was bookish, but it worked for me.

I had the same roommate for all three years. She was not much of a partier either, so we got along nicely. We had been randomly assigned together in the dorm our first year, and it worked out for both of us, so when we moved off campus, we stayed together.

We both studied pretty hard, and both had jobs. I worked at a local bookstore, and she worked over at the university library. I also recently started picking up a few tutoring jobs on the side. It was pretty good cash money and helped me learn the material better myself. A lot of the students were mostly interested in having me write their papers for them, and while they offered a lot of money for it, I refused. I did not need to jeopardize my own future for their convenience.

Almost everywhere I went, I wore loose khaki pants and an oversized sweater.

Some might call the look dowdy or librarian, but I was an English major so what did I care. My hair stayed pulled back in a ponytail, and I was constantly pushing my glasses up my nose.

The teachers loved me because I was always on time, turned in reliably good work, and never made a fuss. I did ask a lot of questions in class, but they did not seem to mind the conversation it usually sparked. Granted, that conversation was usually just between the professor and myself, but I learned a lot.

As the tutoring picked up, I started to cut back on my hours at the bookstore. It was okay with me, I usually spent my whole paycheck in the store so it actually saved me quite a bit of money to focus more on the tutoring. My English professors were starting to recommend me which I took as a high compliment.

By my senior year, I was also the teaching assistant to one of them, Dr. Andrews, at least for her introductory classes. She was encouraging me to continue my studies after college, going for my masters and perhaps a Ph.D. but I just was not sure I wanted to keep studying for the next six or eight years.

One afternoon, I was grading tests when Dr. Andrews approached me about a new tutoring student.

"This one will pay double," she stated.

"Double? Why?"

"Because the student will pay full price and the university will match it."

"What? Why on earth would they do that?"

"It's Thomas Logan."

"Who?"

Dr. Andrews laughed, "Have you ever even been to one of our football games?"

I shook my head, "I usually sign up for work shifts during those times. The bookstore is almost empty, and I can study."

"Oh Laura, you need to get out more," she laughed again, "But anyway, Thomas is the star running back of our team. They predict he will go pro after college, but he's in danger of losing his eligibility to play if he doesn't pass English."

"Ohhh, one of those. He doesn't really care about English, he just wanted to play football."

"Well, I've never met him, so I don't know. But the coach and the dean have worked this out, and our department head recommended you for the tutor."

"Wow, that's great. And I don't mind double payments. How hard can it be to teach a football player how to read?"

Dr. Andrews laughed, "Laura, come now. You have to be nice to him."

I sighed but finally agreed. Double the pay for the same amount of time sounded great to me. At the time, my roommate and I were planning a Spring Break trip to Washington DC for sightseeing, and I was in need of the spending money.

We set up the first session, and I went home to do a little research. I was obviously not into football, but I did not want to appear ignorant in front of this star player. It turns out that the guy was actually doing very well in his math and science classes, just struggled in English. He also grew up in Philadelphia which was where my grandparents lived when I was growing up. Maybe it would not be such a bore after all. And he was not bad on the eyes.

I went into my teaching assistant website and pulled up the syllabus that he would be working on. It looked pretty straightforward to me, but if you are a football player who likes algebra and biology, I can see where it would be boring and possibly difficult.

I checked out some of the books from the library and spent the next few days brushing up on the basics. I had not read some of them in years, and again, I did not want to appear ignorant. Especially not at double the price.

I mentioned to my roommate, Amy, that I was going to tutor Thomas Logan.

"Ohhh, he's kind of sexy," she giggled.

"You know who he is?"

"Yeah, I try to stay up on current events."

I laughed, "I had to look him up."

"And?" she nudged me.

"Well, he's not bad if you like the tall, muscular, brooding types," I laughed.

"Who doesn't!"

In getting ready for the session with Thomas, I have to admit, I did take a little extra care with my shower and makeup. I left my hair down and even managed to squeeze contacts into my eyes. I chose a simple sundress to wear, hoping that it fell into that 'cute but casual' category that seemed too illusive to bookish little me.

Amy gave me a wolf-whistle when I came out of my room.

"I see you found his picture!"

"It's not that!" I protested, "The department chair recommended me for this, and I want to make a good impression."

"Uh huh, because the department chair is interested in that pink lip gloss you have on."

I rolled my eyes and pushed her out the door for her movie.

****

I have to admit, when Thomas showed up, the pictures I had found of him did not do him justice. He was tall and tan, with green eyes and a quick smile.

"Hi, I'm Thomas," he introduced himself politely.

"Laura," I replied, a little nervous to be one on one with the handsome football player.

"You don't look like what I was expecting," he laughed.

"Really? What were you expecting?" I was a little startled by his comment.

"Everyone said you were a librarian type. The guys gave me a hard time about the bookworm."

I chuckled, "Yeah, I don't really dress up for class like the Barbies do."

I did not mean to let that unflattering nickname slip out; it was the name Amy, and I had given the bleached blondes in their tight little sweaters.

Thomas laughed, "Oh hell, that's exactly what they are."

I shrugged, "I guess I'm more interested in school, I don't know."

His eyes studied me closely, "What? No parties and boyfriends?"

"Not really. Never seems to be important I guess."

"Well, I've been doing too much. I need to ace this English exam if I'm going to keep playing."

"Too much partying? From a football player?" I regretted the words as soon as I spoke them.

Luckily Thomas just laughed, "Yeah, I know. But what can I do... Everyone loves a star football player."

"I don't know anything about football," I admitted quietly.

"Then this should work out, I don't know anything about English."

I laughed, "I'm glad you're one of the ones with a sense of humor at least."

We sat down together on the couch to start. He spread out his books and papers all over the coffee table, and I cringed slightly at the mess.

"Where do we start?" he ran his fingers through his thick blonde hair.

"What does this exam cover?"

"Something about Shakespeare I think."

"You think?" I laughed.

"Yeah, I've missed a few classes."

"Have you done the reading at least?"

"Some of it. I think."

"Oh geez," I sighed.

It appears from his syllabus that the test would cover Taming of the Shrew, one of my least favorite Shakespeare works.

"I'm not a fan of this one," I warned him.

"Why's that?"

"If you had read it, you would probably know." I arched one eyebrow at him.

He laughed, "Probably not, Shakespeare is hard to understand."

"How about you start reading, and I'll make us something to eat?"

He nodded and flipped open the book. I headed to the kitchen to fix us some food. I returned about twenty minutes later with a tray of soft chicken tacos, chips, and guacamole. I also brought back several sodas.

"No beer?" he chuckled.

"Not until you finish reading," I wagged a finger at him.

He wrapped his hand around my finger and pulled me to him.

"What?" I struggled to regain my footing.

"There are better uses for such delicate fingers," he winked.

I felt my cheeks flush pink and finally managed to wrestle my finger away.

I sat back down and grabbed a taco to eat while he read.

"I don't understand this shit," he complained.

"It can take some getting used to," I acknowledged.

"Read it with me," he placed the book flat on the coffee table.

I swallowed my last bite of taco and bent over next to him. I was hyper-aware of his thigh pressing against mine, and I tried to focus on the page in front of me instead. It was not working, especially when he brushed against my arm as he reached for a taco.

I tapped the page to bring his attention back to the studying. He chuckled and shook his head.

"You really are wound tight."

"I am not!" I resented being called uptight, even if it was true.

"Seriously, come here," he grabbed my shoulders lightly and turned me so that my back was to him.

His fingers brushed against the nape of my neck lightly as he moved my hair out of the way, and I shivered. But his hands were sure and strong as he massaged my shoulders. I did not want to admit how good it felt.

He rubbed my neck and shoulders for several minutes, and I was relaxing into the stroking when I realized that his hands had moved. His thumbs were still massaging the middle of my back, but his hands were so large that his fingertips were brushing against the outer curve of my breasts. I did not want to appear frigid on top of being uptight, so I tried to ignore it.

Then his fingers started to join in on the massaging.

"Thomas?" I asked quietly.

Instead of a verbal answer, I got an oral one. His lips were soft yet firm as he brushed them against the back of my neck. I felt a shudder trickle down my spine.

"Thomas, c'mon…" I whispered.

"Laura, you need to lighten up and relax," he chuckled as his fingers grew bolder.

His hands now cupped the sides of my breasts and lightly stroked them. When I turned back towards him, he bent down and kissed me. I was startled, but I can't say that it was unpleasant. In fact, he might have been the best kisser I had ever met.

His hand slid back to the nape of my neck, and he held my mouth to his. It had been too long since I had had a boyfriend, and I am afraid my body responded faster than my brain did. I slid my hands up his muscled chest and let his tongue slide between my lips.

"Thomas," I exhaled softly.

"It's ok," he soothed me, pulling me back into the kiss.

His biceps bulged as he lifted me and set me back down on his lap. I could feel a bulge pressing against me, and my hips seemed eager to feel more. They gyrated on their own as his fingernails raked down my upper back.

****

Thomas's hands slid back up, his skin warm against my exposed neck and shoulders. His lips tickled my collarbone as his fingers entwined themselves in the straps of my sundress. He pulled the straps down slightly, exposing just the tops of my breasts.

His tongue left a damp trail as he traced the upper swells peeking out from my dress. I was wriggling on his lap, and the bulge beneath me seemed to continue to grow. His hips were thrusting slightly, but I could not tell if it was intentional or just an urge.

With every thrust of his hips, I could feel my own dampness growing, and I squirmed against his insistent touch. His mouth was moving further and further south as he peeled my dress down. With the tiny straps, I had not put on a bra. His large hands cupped my tits and held them together, creating quite a bit of cleavage.

He grinned up at me as he ran his thumbs over my stiff nipples. They were barely concealed by the edge of the dress, and the hemline of the material tickled my sensitive skin.

"Damn," he breathed, "Who knew these were under those bulky sweaters?"

I giggled, "They're not bad, hmm?"

"Man, if the rest of the guys knew these were hidden in there, they'd be banging down your door…"

"The guys? The football team?"

"Yeah," he chuckled, "we're all suckers for nice tits."

I arched my back and pressed them into his hands, eliciting a pleased groan from the star running back. He pinched the nipples still hidden under my dress, and I gasped.

"Seriously, Laura, you should show these off more," he finally pulled the dress down far enough for them to pop free.

"Show 'em off?" I was confused, I had never really thought of myself as that kind of girl.

"Oh yeah," he leaned over to the coffee table and grabbed his cell phone.

"Wh-Wh-What are you doing?" I felt my cheeks flush in alarm.

"Just one picture, please? I can take it without your face showing…"

"But why?"

"The guys have got to see these, they're great."

I giggled nervously, terrified of him taking topless pictures of me. I finally figured what the hell, if he could keep my face out, no one would know it was me. The flash snapped brightly, and he flipped the phone around to show me that indeed my face was cropped out.

"Now what?" I shrugged.

He clicked on the phone for a long moment, still grinding his hips up into me.

"There, I sent it to a few friends," he grinned proudly.

"What? Why?" I was horrified.

"You seem, ahem, like you could use a few dates."

"What do you mean?"

He answered by digging his fingers into my hips and pulling my groin down against his. I guess my moans had given me away.

The phone buzzed on the couch, and he glanced down to check the message.

"You might have some more students tonight," he winked.

I stared down ay my bouncing tits and back up at his face. "What? Like this?"

"Oh, exactly like this. And maybe more…"

He took my hand and pressed it to the bulge underneath my body.

"Feel that?"

He moaned as I squeezed his cock gently and nodded.

"I'm on the average size in the locker room…"

My eyes widened at his implications, and I felt a fresh surge of heat to my pussy. I guess my hips must have twitched because he laughed.

"I wasn't wrong, was I?"

I flushed deep pink and shook my head. His fingers were still on top of mine, and he guided my palm up and down his length. Just as I was imagining feeling the warm pulsing flesh, there was a loud knocking at the front door and on instinct, I tried to yank my dress back up but barely managed to cover my nipples.

"Come on in," Thomas invited.

"What? Who is it?"

"The guys," he grinned.

"What? But what about your English exam?"

"We'll study later. Plus, you can make some sweet dough from tutoring all of us. Come on in!" he ended with a hollered invitation.

The door opened before I had a chance to scramble off Thomas's lap, and the three guys strolled in as though they owned the place.

"Damn bro," the tall black guy grinned, "started without us?"

I was surprised that the flesh was still on my face from the burning heat.

"Laura? You might know Andre, Pete, and Mike," he gestured to the trio.

"N-N-No, not really," I admitted shyly.

"This is your tutor? How's the oral exam?" the redhead was grinning widely.

I rolled my eyes at the juvenile humor.

"We're about to find out," Thomas laughed, "but she's a little shy."

"The bookworm? Shy?" the muscular redhead laughed.

"I'm Andre," the black guy introduced himself as he sat down next to Thomas and me.

"And I'm Mike," the Italian-looking one, taking the seat on the other side.

"What about me?" the redhead whined.

"Well, you can have the chair for your bad jokes, Pete."

Thomas pulled me down close to his chest and whispered in my ear, "Just stay right there and focus on me. Pay them no attention, okay?"

I nodded and nuzzled my face into his neck. He slowly peeled the dress back down to my waist and I heard one of the guys suck in their breath sharply and exhale with a low curse. My breasts were pressed up against Thomas's chest so that just the side curves were visible to the other guys.

With one hand firmly on my waist to hold me in place, Thomas's other hand snaked down in between our bodies and slowly stroked my pussy through my underwear.

His voice was soft as his warm breath tickled my ear, "I think you like what's about to happen."

I gasped softly when his fingers found my swollen little clit through the wet silk of my panties. His tiny light circles made my breath catch in my throat, and he slid his mouth across my jawline to my mouth to muffle my moans.

When his finger slipped just inside the hem of my panties and found the same swollen nub, I felt my body shiver. His touch was warm and firm as he expertly dragged me along the edge of pleasure. When his teeth sunk into my neck and his fingers pressed perfectly against me, my whole body shook and shivered as I soaked his fingers with my climax.

"Damn bro," Andre repeated his earlier comment.

I looked up from Thomas's warm neck directly into to Andre's chiseled grinning face and coal black eyes. And without any prompting, I leaned over and kissed his inviting lips. He cupped the back of my head, letting his tongue delve between my lips as I writhed against Thomas's fingers still inside my panties. Thomas teased my sensitive clit lightly, making sure my pussy was already ready for my next explosion.

I felt movement behind me as two strong hands pulled me away from Thomas's body and Andre's mouth, exposing my firm ripe tits. It must have been Pete because Mike was still sitting on the couch, staring hungrily at my quaking body.

Andre and Mike descended on my nipples simultaneously, while Thomas's fingers slipped easily into my pussy. Pete groaned loudly at the sight of my head back as all three football players teased my willing flesh.

"Oh fuck yeah," Pete breathed as his hands slid around to cup underneath my tits, holding them up to the tormenting tongues.

It was quickly becoming too much for my body to take, and I had to distract myself. I shivered as I pulled away from all three and grinned around the room.

"I'd hate to think I'm the only one who brought something to this party," I giggled.

Thomas pressed my hand against his crotch again as Andre promptly unzipped his jeans. His swollen dark cock eagerly bobbed free. He was not as thick as Thomas felt but was very long. I wrapped my delicate pale fingers around his dark flesh and marveled at the sight. The low deep groan he gave me told me he liked it too. I stroked him with a loose grip, teasing him the way he had teased me.

"Oh damn," he groaned, trying to thrust his hips into my grip for more friction.

I tickled his balls with my fingernails before releasing him altogether. His dick bounced against his lower abs in frustration.

I beckoned to Mike on the other side, and he produced his cock for my approval as well. He was much shorter than Andre but nicely thick. I gave him the same light teasing strokes until he was grunting and threatening to finish the job himself.

Pete was still behind me, kneading my tits and thumbing my nipples. I pulled my body away from him and stood up in the middle of all four. With my ass facing poor Thomas and my tits facing the kneeling Pete, I slowly slid the rest of my dress down to the floor. When I stepped out of it and my flip-flops, I was left in nothing but a pair of very wet white silk panties.

The kneeling redhead, Pete, looked up at me and slowly dragged the damp underwear off so that I was completely naked. Suddenly, from all sides, I felt eight hands on my skin. I jumped and shivered and squirmed as they explored my body thoroughly. They were touching my legs, my arms, my back, my tits, and my ass, everywhere but my aching pussy.

"Strip," I breathily ordered the guys.

You have never seen clothing go flying as fast as it did right then. There were shirts and jeans and boxer shorts going everywhere. I felt warm flesh surrounding me as the guys manhandled my body back onto the couch.

I found myself on all fours over Thomas's prone body with Pete kneeling behind me. Standing next to me were Andre and Mike.

"God she's so ready for us," Pete moaned from behind me, his fingers sliding through my wetness.

I heard a strange ripping noise and then suddenly a sheathed cock was sliding inside my pussy. Thomas pulled my face down to his and kissed me roughly, nipping my tongue and nearly bruising my lips. My moans were stifled with his mouth as Pete pounded into me.

"Oh shit, shit, shit," he muttered pretty quickly.

Andre chuckled, "Minuteman."

Pete slung a 'fuck you' at him as his whole body stiffened and then collapsed. He clamored off the couch, and Mike took his position.

Mike's hands were surprisingly gentle as he cupped my ass and held me still for his cock. I pressed my body back against the thick head of his covered cock, and with one quick stroke, he was buried inside me to the hilt.

"Oh damn, she is tight," he groaned, his thrusts fast and hard.

Andre laughed, "Damn white guys."

I was bucking against Mike, squeezing him with those inner muscles until his whole body went rigid like Pete's and then he was softening inside me.

I slid my hand down Thomas's quivering stomach to feel his perfect cock ready for me. He was nicely thick and perfectly long, and that was what I wanted next. I motioned for Andre to move closer and Thomas quickly wrapped his cock in protection. I finally sat up and eased myself down onto his shaft with Andre grinning at me, stroking his own cock until I got my bearings.

When I reached for that long dark shaft, Andre slid it smoothly into my tight little fist until the head bumped against my waiting lips. I wrapped my warm wet mouth around the head and let my tongue swirl around the sensitive head.

"Oh fuck," Andre groaned. Mike and Pete both laughed as his instant reaction.

Thomas's cock stretched me as it slid slowly in and out, distracting me from sucking Andre. I took a deep breath and slid my mouth as far down that length as it would go, letting my hand engulf the rest. With long wet strokes, I willed Andre to cum for me. I flicked my tongue against the sensitive underside fast and firm, finding every little ridge and vein.

"Oh damn," he groaned, yanking his hips backwards to withdraw his cock.

With just a few more strokes aimed at my tits, my hand finished him off, and I was soon covered with the jets of his cock.

Andre quickly wiped them off with his large palms, and I turned to face Thomas.

"Hello again," he laughed.

"Where have you been?" I giggled.

His hips thrust up hard, "Here."

My breath caught in my throat, and my head fell back.

"Oh like that," I moaned.

He pounded up into me, as hard and as fast as he could move. My whole body was bouncing, the other three guys staring at my tits and ass as Thomas made them jiggle and shimmy.

"Fuck her, Tom," one of them spurred him on, "make her cum."

Thomas was doing a damn good job of that. With every thrust, I could feel our bodies collide, sending me closer to the edge. His fingers dug into my hips and held me just an inch or so above his groin. With fast hard plunges, he shoved me over the cliff. I screamed something unintelligible and felt my body squeeze his cock tightly.

"Oh goddamn," he hollered as he stiffened and exploded inside me.

I finally collapsed on top of him, and I passed out.

****

When Thomas and I woke up a few hours later, we were curled up under a blanket together, and the other three were nowhere to be found. He helped me to the shower and even bathed me, taking great care with my sore body.

After that night, I went out with each of those guys a couple of times but ended up actually dating Thomas for a long time. My roommate was completely baffled by my new behavior, but the looks I got on campus in my little sundress with Thomas's arm around my waist were truly priceless.

Oh and the English exam? Thomas passed with flying colors.

I Have a Surprise.

Freya's phone call caught me completely unprepared, perhaps because I considered the relationship, I had with her completely casual and without any possibility of having a future. Instead, Brett's sister wanted to invite me, with the excuse of having passed my bar examination with flying colors, for 'an evening celebration at her house, in which 'I would have had a pleasant surprise'.

I decided that I too would give her a surprise, so after completely shaving my pussy, I wore nothing under my usual elasticized minidress, and it was only because I was still without a car that forced me to cover myself with a light duster before to take a taxi to go to his house. She welcomed me in her usual sensual way, wrapped in a dress very similar to mine as far as size was concerned.

"You always look more beautiful every time I see you," she told me before giving me a long kiss in the mouth.

"You're not missing any steps either, you always look amazing," I replied, sliding my hand from my neck to her side, touching her breast.

She took me by the hand to take me to the living room, where a handsome man, about thirty years old, dressed to the nines, was waiting for us on a large sofa.

"This is Hayden, a dear friend of mine," Freya told me.

"I don't think it's just a friend," I replied, "but I think he will be kind enough to lend me his tie."

He said nothing but took off the tie; which, he passed me, and with which I tied

Freya's wrists very gently to a radiator.

"So, you can get rid of it whenever you want." I said giving her a kiss in the mouth "But I know you will wait for me to call you."

Very naturally, I took off the duster, and immediately afterward I pulled my dress to the ground and remained completely naked, before going to sit next to Hayden, who greeted me and immediately gave me a kiss in the mouth.

"In your opinion, how long will you be able to stay there," I asked the man after taking a hand from him that I placed on my genitals.

"I don't know, but if you continue like this I will explode," he replied, bringing his other hand to my breast.

We began to kiss each other with increasing passion, while his hands flowed on every pore of my skin. I touched myself to excite Freya as much as possible, who was already beginning to give little signs that she was hot.

Slowly I turned to Hayden to open his shirt. I then stood up, putting myself between his legs.

"Do you like me," I asked, brushing his lips with my finger.

He didn't answer me, but he put his lips on my moist flower and kissed her, sucking the lips with enthusiasm. When he turned me around, I leaned forward on a small table, thus offering him my beautiful ass. He took the opportunity to kiss my little hole before licking it, slowly turning his tongue around, to take a sip my moods.

I looked over at Freya, despite being tied up, she was touching herself with more and more insistence, but I didn't want to end the sweet torture to which I had condemned her. So, I crawled on the couch to continue offering myself to Hayden, who continued to lick my intimacy, paying no attention to the hostess in any way.

"Turn around and open your legs, I want all of you," Hayden told me, giving me a small slap on the butt.

I obeyed, sliding on to the sofa until I was sitting with my buttocks on the edge, holding my ankles with my hands. He opened the little hole a finger, then slipped his tongue in, followed a little later by another finger. In response, I had him lick two fingers, which then ended immediately inside my wet hole.

"Please, untie me, I can't stand it anymore," Freya told me, now at the height of her excitement.

"If you want me to, I will, but as a punishment, there will only be anal," I replied, while Hayden sodomized me with two fingers.

She freed herself of the tie and then took off her dress under which she wore only a purple lace thong and sat by my side. Our mouths found each other immediately, as did our tongues that sought each other out in an endless game.

"To this, I think," she said, taking my fingers out of my pussy to put her own into it.

"Maybe it's better for me to do it," Hayden replied, slipping off his pants and boxers, showing off an erection of respectable size.

Excited as I was, that beautiful bat slipped into me without finding any resistance.

"I like it," I said moaning in a moment when Freya let me free my mouth. "Let me enjoy this like you belong to me and are here for my pleasure and nothing else."

Freya then took off her thong to lie on top of me in the classic sixty-nine position, and with great surprise, I saw that she had a plug well planted in her ass.

"You're more of a whore than I am without my pants," I told her, taking out her plug to be able to lick her anus and play with her ass.

"It's true, but for now you keep his cock warm for me," I pushed Hayden back to have Freya suck on his penis.

I found myself face-to-face with Freya's ass. Freya; meanwhile, was completely taken by sucking Hayden's cock, and as usual, I could not resist the temptation to give her a mixture of pain and pleasure. So, I took the plug between my fingers and started inserting it lightly, which despite its small size, was able to dilate the anus considerably. At the same time, I began to gently massage her clitoris, knowing that this would be the maximum pleasure I would allow her to receive from the whole vagina this night.

"Now, let us see how much your girlfriend has enlarged it," Hayden said, moving Freya onto the sofa and then standing behind her.

Acting as a true dominant male, he removed the plug to take her immediately after, making his cock disappear inside her with a few powerful lunges.

"Ouch so you hurt me," she protested weakly.

"Shut up, as if you didn't know that in less than a minute you will be begging me to go harder as you're on the door of ecstasy."

In fact, Freya's moans soon became a clear signal that she was enjoying everything, so all I could do was try to get my strap on quickly. But as soon as I tried to move, Hayden stopped me to let Freya rise above me.

"Lick her," He ordered me authoritatively.

"Yes sir," I replied smiling for a moment, before finding Freya's moist lake in front of my face.

I don't know if I was more excited to have her tongue between my legs or to see her taking it anally like a little whore, with Hayden banging her without any restraint, thinking only of his own pleasure. Despite this, Freya had an orgasm that left her breathless, even if for a short while as I pushed her, making her fall on the sofa to take her place.

Hayden didn't say a word, nor was there any need for it, but he stood behind me to resume fucking me with unexpected calm. Besides, it was enough for me to slide his large erection into my moist clam to experience an almost absolute pleasure, soon made even bigger by Freya's tongue that licked every corner of my intimate lips. When he slid back a little, I realized he was coming, so I turned to receive the fruit of his pleasure directly at the source, taking all of him into my mouth. Hayden squirted violently into my mouth, which I then released in Freya's who was waiting to play with me a little.

"If you want, I'll take you home," Hayden asked me while we were dressing.

"Thanks, it'll save me some cab fare," I replied, very happy not to have to spend money to go home.

"But only if you put this on," he told me, pointing to the plug Freya had used.

So, I took the small wedge, and after giving it some licking to lubricate it, I slipped it into my rectum without saying a single word.

On the journey to my home, we talked of nothing but Freya and her sexual tastes, of which Hayden knew much more than me as he had been frequenting her for years. While he spoke, his hand lingered long on my legs, but without ever reaching the vagina that was almost exposed by the shortness of my dress.

Once at my front door, he wanted to follow me with the excuse of not leaving me alone in the middle of the street, but once inside the hall of the building, his attitude changed rapidly.

"What's behind there," he asked, pointing to a small space under the stairs.

"Nothing at the moment there is only a table that someone has left. I'm guessing someone was supposed to pick it up."

He grabbed me by the arm sort of forcefully taking me to that little nook under the stairs. He leaned me over the table and raised my dress so he could get to my ass.

"What do you think, can anyone see us here," I asked, hoping to soften him.

"If anyone sees you, he will only know that he has a neighbor who is a bit of a slut," he replied, lowering his pants and showing me his cock already at full erection.

In a moment of pity, after having removed the plug I had in my ass without delicacy, he spat on the hole a couple of times and then let in the saliva using a finger.

"Now, you see that you don't shout otherwise you will wake up your looky-loo neighbors."

He sodomized me with the same force used with Freya, sliding the whole of himself into me with an almost maddening rhythm, and luckily, I managed not to scream despite the first immediate throws of pain I had felt before the pleasure began.

"You're just a slut who pretends to be a respectable woman," he said pulling me by the hair "An ass to take before others do."

"Then take it as you see fit," I replied in pride "Also because I like it and you don't know how much."

Hayden forced me to get down on the floor on all fours and started to fuck me like before, but this time I reached out a hand that I brought to my dripping wetness to masturbate without any restraint.

"You like to take it in the ass, don't you bitch!"

"Shut up, I'm enjoying it."

I don't know how long he sodomized me on the floor, but then it was clear that he was a real bull, an alpha male from his very being. As it was evident that I enjoyed perhaps even more than him, masturbating without stopping while he penetrated me with all the strength he had in his body. In the end, he came deep inside me.

"Wait till I clean myself," he said wiping himself off using my dress. Then, as he put the plug back into my ass he said, "and now you can go home."

I saw him walk away as I stood up, trying to put the dress back in place so as to cover at least the lower parts. With my legs still shaking, I managed to get back to my apartment and immediately throw myself in the shower, as I had felt a little dirty, although maybe it was just to freshen up my ideas. However, I now understood how Lara or Freya must have felt when I treated them the same way that Hayden had used me. As a body to use at will.

I wondered if I really wanted to follow that road made of occasional relationships, in which I could be used by brutal men just to please them, or where I could be the dominator and not just women of a submissive nature. Maybe it was better to stay with people like Jasmine, and partly even Amber, for whom sex was just a diversion during which they always kept some control. I decided it was better to have a good night's sleep and to postpone my thoughts for another day.

A Long Convention Day

Gabe was scratching his head ... It was the middle of a long convention day. He wanted to help, but he didn't know much about the design of the cosplay or the sewing repair, but he needed his help. With the top half-on and half-off, she held up her arm again.

"You see?" she asked. "It doesn't want to stay on!" she said at this point.

Chel was a bit of a spitfire when she was resurrected about something. She could be with the best of them, too. Gabe wished that his daughter, Chel's best friend, was here. She knew what she was doing, and she could find out how to fix the problem with the dress.

But then again, if she were here, Gabe probably wouldn't have had the half-naked wonder in front of him. Chel was wearing a skirt that was part of the outfit. The blouse, a little school-girl number, hung half of her as she held one arm in her sleeve. Below, there was a skimpy lace dress. Chel was all 5 '4 "tall and had very little to the neck. Obviously, the bra was more conservative than supportive. When she turned to reveal the sleeve problem from another perspective, Gabe had to see her butt in the picture. That was one thing she could certainly brag about.

Both his daughter and Chel talked to him about coming to this convention. Gabe's wife was there, too. Actually, his wife knew the effect that little Chel had on him. She worked her deft magic to take advantage of the 'cosplay emergency' and devised a way for Gabe to be alone in the hotel room with Chel. I owe her this, he thought as he admired the curve of her tight little ass.

"I just don't know what to do about it, Chel," he said. "If the arm goes down, I guess all we can do is put it on. Neither of you has brought a sewing machine.

He glanced at his watch. "It's getting kind of late. Why don't you turn into one of your other outfits so that we can get back to the con before it closes? "He knew he had a lot of time, and his wife would have kept his daughter occupied long enough for him to enjoy some time oblivious to this little pert minx. Does she know the effect she has on her? He wondered.

Chel sighed as only an 18-year-old girl could and let the rest of the top slide off her arm. She crossed her arms in front of her bra-covered chess and looked down. "I guess so ..." she said and trailed off, obviously disappointed that her cosplay plans weren't working as she had hoped. He took a step towards her, careful not to get too close and make her uncomfortable. I know you wanted to wear this one, but you just don't have a choice.

She looked up, and he could say that she was closer to tears than he thought the situation was calling for. He cocked his head and asked, "Chel, are you OK? Looks like something else is bothering you, what's up?"

She took a deep breath and reached out to put her hand over his "There's nothing ... I'm just ..." she shrugged. "Frustrated, I guess. Nothing ever seems to be going right." She squeezed his hand, slipped out of it, and moved over to sit on the bed. She reached down and pulled the suitcase that contained her other outfits to her. She hopped out of bed long enough to slip off her skirt and sat back down. Gabe was grateful that at the time, her back was to him so that he could change the rising erection to make it less noticeable.

Chel's pants matched her bra. Both in red and black lace that reflected the purity that she still seemed to radiate. Have I wrongly named her? He was curious.

She unzipped the suitcase and lifted the top of it. She stopped and raised another sigh. Gabe watched as she fell to the top of the suitcase, and floated over to her side, with her back still on her.

Gabe walked over and sat on the edge of the bed next to her, putting his hand back on her shoulder. "What's wrong?" he asked, rubbing his thumb against her ear.

"There's nothing ..." she closed her eyes. "All, I just ... uuuggggggggg."

He grabbed her shoulder and started rubbing up and down the top of her neck. "What? Tell me," he said.

"This whole thing about the dress... I haven't had a good time because I miss my husband... me and Mel had a battle..."

"Wait ..." he stopped rubbing her when his friend, Mel, was listed. "Who were you and Mel fighting for?"

Chelsea's eyes widened and a dark flush spread over her cheeks. "Um ... nothing, never mind it." She kept looking away and twisted a little more to cover her face.

It must have been humiliating, whatever it was, he thought. Was it a question of ... Me, huh? He rejected the idea ... His attraction to her blurred the moment with the fantasies of her professing a lustful desire for him. He shook his head and pushed it forward.

"Ok ... I'm going to forget about it. But as far as your boyfriend goes, that's part and parcel of a long-distance relationship." He knew her boyfriend was living on the other side of the country.

She sighed again. "I know, I'm just ..."

He continued to stroke her arm.

"It's just ... Masturbation is just going so far," she sighed, covering her face further.

Gabe was stunned by the silence. He had the visions that were starting out like this. She trusts him with sexual issues. One thing that leads to another ... He cleared his throat and continued stroking his neck, reaching from the top of his shoulder to his wrist, running his fingertips softly over his skin. He could see that the goosebumps were breaking out on her.

"Do you think he's going to let you ... ahem ... take care of the needs? I know some long-distance relationships are open like that."

"We talked about it," she said, her words coming a little easier now that she broke the ice. "He said it's all right, but only if it's all right for both of us ... like ... we can both play around."

"Is that it?" he asked. "Okay, I mean, with both of you?"

"I don't know ... I haven't been really thrilled about it before, but it's been harder and harder to ignore my own needs."

Gabe extended his stroking to include the top of her shoulder and neck. She turned her head to expose a little more of her neck. He thought he heard a faint sigh from her, but that may have been his imagination.

"So ... have you been talking about it? Playing?" he asked.

"I ... um ... kinda." She seemed reluctant to give details about this. But as his first fingers slipped into her hairline, he heard a certain soft moan, and she turned to her stomach.

"What's stopping you?" he asked, trailing his fingers down her back. He feathered them along her spine, fighting the urge to unplug her bra. He was happy to see more goose bumps and a slight squirm in her hips

"I don't know ... I'm not sure who I should play with," she said. And then, more quietly, "Hmm, that feels good."

Encouraged, he let his fingers go down to the top of his panties. Once, he had to struggle for balance in order not to force them down. As it was, he marvelled at the sight of her young, tight ass.

"What would you have been looking for if you were going to?"

"Um ... someone who's all right with just playing, I think. I don't want a relationship ... we 're not poly. Someone who knows what they're doing. If I play, I want it to be ... uh ... worth it?"

He curled his fingers and applied soft scratching to his back stroking. Once, he was rewarded with a soft moan.

He's been quiet for a minute. He couldn't believe that he had gotten this far away. Here was this adorable little nymph who unknowingly (he thought?) mocked him after he was his daughter's best friend. This innocent little thing that he had been willing to do just what he was doing right now ... Simply, asking him what she wanted and what she needed ... It was HIM.

He hoped that he would read all the signs correctly. He kept his fingers and fingernails running up and down from deep into her long hair, all the way down to the top of her panties. As she kept making her little mews of pleasure, he went back to what she had written ... He didn't want to make any mistake and destroy not only her love for him, but also make things weird to his daughter. He took a deep breath and plunged.

"You know, I could, uh ... help you with that ..."

She was nervous, and he was afraid of the worst.

Slowly, she turned on her back and gazed up at him. Her eyes are a mixture of doubt, trepidation, and (he hoped) desire. "You mean, huh?"

He had the best look of care and relaxed confidence that he could manage; "Yeah, I could help you play." He put his hand on her bare stomach, but he didn't push it. She didn't make a move to push her away.

"I ..." she began, but she trailed off.

He grinned gently at her, and made a tiny circle with his hand on her stomach at every point: "I don't want a partnership ... I have one. I know what I'm doing ... ask my wife. And, I will make it worth it." Although he tried to maintain a cool, confident look on his face, his heart was pounding. He jumped across a line that could not have been uncrossed.

"But your mom, will she be ... OK with that?"

Yes , yes! He was listening. She doesn't say no! He tried to keep a relaxed smile from his face as he knew that she was working on problems that would prevent her from saying yes. "Her and I are in an open relationship. We 're not poly, we 're just playing with other men." He trailed his fingers from one side of his ribs to the other. Up and down between the bottom of her bra and the rest of her pants.

"I 'm ... I don't ..." She looked in his eyes all this time, but now she looked away. Slowly, he shifted his hand to the top of her bra and gave a soft caress to her pert breast. She closed her eyes and arched her hand so slightly. "But what of Mel?"

"What about her? What I do, and what you do is none of her business," he answered. He let go of her breast, trailed down her fingers, and wrapped them around her panties over her mound. He could tell that she shaved because of how thin they were. No wisp of hair could be detected through the fabric. By this point, his cock was as hard as a rock.

She kept her eyes closed and moved her hips slightly in time with her fingers. She wasn't trying to move further under his hand, but he got a message. He slipped his fingertips between my thighs, feeling the shape of my lips through my thin panties.

She drew in a breath and arched her back again. "Well?" he said. "Do you want to use me to take care of your needs?" he kept his fingers moving gradually between his thighs, sliding the other from his breast, to his throat, and running his thumb across his cheeks.

She began to push a little more, but Gabe could still feel some resistance. She had not yet given herself to him. He thought for a moment and remembered some of the conversations he had heard between Chel and Mel. He remembers that she was interested in being tied up, spanked, generally submissive. He was struck by a spark of inspiration.

He bent down next to his ear. He cut her pussy and inserted his fingers into her hair. "Or ... I might just take you ..." he squeezed a fist full of her hair as he said, "Take it." That was it, man.

She shuddered from head to toe, and he could feel the surge of her panties. Sweetly, she whimpered, snapped open her eyes and looked straight at him. In her eyes, there was a mixed look of excitement and fear. He had it, he knew it.

"I ..." she said. He growled, tugged her hair, and pressed his mouth tightly against hers. Her arms came up against his chest, but there was no strength behind them. She began rubbing her soaked pussy against his hand as he forced his tongue into her mouth. Her moans went back and forth from lustful to terrified.

He grabbed her pussy tightly through her panties and moved her mouth to her ear. He said to her, "It's all right, little one ... you don't have to make the choice. I'll make it for you."

He put her on her back and straddled her legs to prevent her from getting up (not that she was trying hard). He leaned back and forth, kissing and licking up and down her spine before unplugging her bra. He pulled it violently from beneath her, forcing her to get up for a moment. He caught a glimpse of her tiny breasts in the mirror across the room. His cock grew even harder in the sight of her topless, and her eyes closed with pleasure.

"Hmm," he growled, moving back to the hand between her thighs. She was totally flooded. "You don't want that, don't you?" she whimpered, but said nothing. "Answer me!" he asked, and he grabbed a handful of her hair again.

"Yes!" she said, her breaths coming quickly. "Please , please!"

He was standing next to the bed, still on her back, holding her there. He removed his belt and let his pants fall to the floor. He dragged her to the edge of the bunk, still lying on her stomach. He lifted her head up by pulling her hair with one hand and raising her chin with the other. "Open your mouth," he said.

She opened her eyes and saw the hard cock sticking out, pointing straight at her. Her eyes narrowed, and she opened her mouth as wide as she could. Gabe 's cock wasn't so big, maybe just shy of 6 inches. But he had never received any complaints.

He pulled her head tight to her hair and mouth, and slipped the tip of his cock past her lips. He noticed like her tongue was circling around her head and noticed like she was sucking some of it in. She let out a muffled moan as he put more of his cock in her mouth. She made little grunts while building a slow , steady rhythm to fuck her face.

He relaxed his hold on her hair and played through her fingertips, telling her, "Hmm, good girl." Her praise increased her efforts, and she added more movement of her head to her work.

Gabe let her go on for a couple of minutes, petting her head as she was serving him. But he could already feel his balls tightening up. He pushed his head back and pulled his cock out of his mouth. She was puffing for breath and laid her head back down. Before she could calm herself down, Gabe grabbed her and flipped her back and spun around her. She yelled in surprise.

Gabe pulled off his shirt, leaned over her, and kissed her again. This time, she came back eagerly with a kiss, her tongue slipping into her mouth this time. She reached out to both arms around his back and pulled him down. He swallowed a chuckle at her excitement.

He reached back and pulled her arms around him. She looked as if she was shocked, until he raised both of them over her head and held them tightly there. She had the notion, and she writhed playfully against his hold. He kissed her again, moving out of her mouth, over her ear, and down her face. She moaned and whimpered as he kissed her way down her collarbone to her breasts. He paused for a moment to admire the beautiful little beauty that was held underneath him. He was appreciative of her tiny breasts with perky little nipples. He grinned and hit one of them.

She arched up again to allow him better access as he bit, biting one nipple first, then the other. He took both of her wrists in one hand and slipped the other down to one breast. He gave her a squeeze while sucking the other one, and kept his hand down to her panties. He grabbed one side of it and ripped it off. Again, she gasped and squirmed against his grip.

He put his hand on her now bare pussy and rubbed it gently as he kissed her stomach. He was reluctant to let go of her hands as his reach stretched out as soon as he approached her mound. He smelled her excitement as he got closer to her. He felt her fingers entwined in his hair as she gently pushed him down. Once, from bottom to top, he kissed his way to her slit and licked his tongue around her clit. He slipped his finger inside her as he kept licking. She moaned long and loud as she kept licking and fingering her pussy. She tasted as sweet as he thought she was. He lapped the juices that poured freely from her. He felt it tight, and a fresh gush filled his mouth. He smiled as she grabbed her hair tightly in her first orgasm of the day. But, not the last one, he told himself.

"P — Please — I ..." she panted, trying to catch her breath. He made his way back to her body, trying to avoid more sensitive areas for the moment. He kissed her lips, then her nose as she continued to breathe. Before he could kiss her lips again, she opened her eyes and stared at him. "Please, please fuck me ..." she pleaded.

She stretched out her hand along his chest, down his stomach, and grabbed his cock. "Please, I need this inside of me!" he said, not wanting to keep her waiting, rose and knelt between her legs. She spread her knees wide and revealed herself to him. She was so breathtakingly cute. It's so small ... Well, so vulnerable ... It's so innocent-looking.

She squeezed his cock a little more firmly until he could respect her for a long time.

"Please, please!"

He moved forward again, and she helped him line up his cock with the opening. She rubbed her head up and down her slit a few times, then removed her cock and put her arms on her hips. He took over keeping his cock in place as she pulled him in to get in. He was trying to enjoy this moment ... He had been dreaming about it (literally, sometimes) for so long. He kept his eyes on her face as he put his cock 's head against her and slowly pushed in.

As he slowly relaxed into her, she closed her eyes tightly and tilted her head back. "Oooohhh fuuuuck yeeeess," she said in a long moan as he slid into her, inch by inch. Once inside her, he closed his own eyes and enjoyed the incredible silk tightness of her pussy. He held himself still, fully inside of her, and savored it. As she began to raise her hands, he opened his eyes and looked down at her. She smiled lustfully at him and shocked him with "Finally, I've been waiting for you to fuck me for a long time now. I told Mel that I thought you were hot," she said with a grin. "And I bet you've got a big cock. That's what we've been fighting for," she said.

It shocked him for a moment that she was searching for him, too. She's always played such an innocent little girl. For the time being, he put that out of his mind and got to work. He slid his cock in and out of her at a steady pace. He leaned down, locked his lips on hers, and they kissed deeply. The kiss was full of tongues and moaning. She broke the kiss and started to moan louder.

"I 'm going to cum again," she said. He kept his pace for a moment, and when she began to breathe more quickly, he stopped. She took a surprised look at him, and saw him laughing. "Not yet, little man," he said. He sat up and turned her back on her stomach. He reached down to her hips and pulled her ass up. He lined up his cock and slipped back into her pussy in a single stroke. She moaned out at the doorway and grunted with every thrust he gave her. He fucked her very hard from behind ... To take her as he promised. He didn't stop this time until she cried out that she was cumming again. He pushed his cock all the way in, holding it up, kissing the back of her neck and shoulders.

Once she slowed her breath back down, he gently turned her back again. He slipped between her legs and kissed her sweetly. He slid his cock back in, savoring the feeling of getting into her tight pussy. This time, they fucked each other in a slow, relaxed pace, kissing and nibbling. She looked up at him with a helpless smile on her face (Damn, she 's good at that act! he thought) and asked, "Can you make me cum again? Please?" She put on the face of a perfectly innocent little girl ... Goddamn it for the first time. It almost put him on the brink.

He ground his teeth and regained control of it. He grunted his assent and began to fuck her faster and harder. To his astonishment, she had a sweet , innocent look on her face all the time. "Please, Mr. Gabe, please make me cum again," she said.

It didn't take a long time. "I think I'm going to ... Oh my God!" she exclaimed as she came back again. Gabe had hit the edge of his boundaries this time. He hurled harder and harder until he felt the cum boiling up his cock. He pulled out, and with only one stroke, blast cum up her stomach, across her pussy little tits, and on her sweet, puffy face.

He was grunting and moaning, so he didn't hear the door open to the hotel room. "Chel?! Daddy?! WHAT THE FUCK?!"

Gabe glanced at the door of the hotel room to see the flash of his daughter's skirt as she raced out of the door and back down the hall. His wife leaned against the door frame, her arms folded across her breasts, and a knowing smile on her face. "Hmm ..." was all she could do for a moment as she took a cock in her hand in the sight of her friend, bending over this delicate little nymph coated in his cum. Chel was still floating from her climax.

"You, ah, might want to get dressed and go work with your daughter," said his wife, walking into the house. She reached behind her, untied her clothes, and made her way to the bed. "I'm going to stay here and ... clean up this one." A little whimper from the bed indicated that she had been noticed by Chel and knew EXACTLY what she said.

Sinful sex

The phone rang incessantly. Wondering why Lana didn't answer it, I rolled over, searching blindly for the receiver.

"Hello," I mumbled.

"Wake up, Ryan. Wake up!" Her voice was strident.

"Who is it?"

"Mary Jane. Do you know where Lana is?"

I looked around.

Where the hell was Lana?

"Ryan!" Mary Jane shouted. "It's two thirty in the morning. Where is your wife?"

"I don't know."

"I do. She's at Bart's house pulling a train. Do you know what that means? She's gangbanging all your so-called friends. You're a laughing stock. A cuckold too stupid to know his wife is cuckolding him. Wake up, Ryan!"

"I am awake."

"No, you're not. Everyone knows about her but you, and everyone who knows her does her. Do you like being married to the biggest slut in town?" she said, her voice low and cold.

"No."

"That's what she is. She did Bart the night before your wedding. She did some guy she met on the beach while you were on your honeymoon and bragged about it when she got back. Now she's doing all of them. How does that make you feel?"

"Shitty," I said. "Really low and shitty."

"Maybe there's hope for you yet," she replied. "Good night, Ryan. I'll pray for you," she said before hanging up.

In less than a minute, I was dressed and running for the car. In less than ten minutes, I tried Bart's front door, but it was unlocked. I quietly let myself in and tiptoed to the living room. A bunch of them were sitting around naked, drinking beer and sho o ting the shit.

There was Bart in his easy chair—one of my two best friends. A groomsman at our wedding. I knew Bart would fuck anything, but I thought he'd leave my wife alone out of friendship if nothing else. His wife, Betty, was a sweet and giving woman. I liked her, but she was a certified slut. Hell, I slept with her before she dated Bart and she had offered herself to me regularly since then. I knew they were wife swappers because both of them had approached me about Lana and me joining their club.

There were my other friends—Andy, Bill, Jack, Little Jeff and Pete.

Betty, wearing a sweatshirt that covered everything to her crotch, came in from the kitchen with two beers in each hand. She saw me and froze. "Hello, Ryan," she said.

The room got deathly quiet. I looked at each of them, but they wouldn't look at me.

"Where's Lana?" I asked.

"In the bedroom with Big Jeff and Mike," Betty replied.

Just then Mike came through the door from the hall. "Next," he announced with a big shit-eating grin. He saw me and sagged back against the wall with his mouth hanging open. Mike—my other best friend and brother-in-law. I knew Amy, my sister, didn't know about her husband fucking the town slut. Amy would cut off Mike's nuts if she knew.

"Don't blame us. We're not the only ones she's fucking," Bill said.

"Yeah, Ryan. If she's giving it away, why shouldn't your friends get some? She's the best I've ever had," Bart added. Betty looked pissed off, but the guys mumbled in agreement.

Bart was right. Lana was built like a brick shithouse and had a wild, demanding sensuality when she wanted sex, which was a lot of the time. She'd get a look in her eye—a supernatural look like in a cartoon. No man could resist that look. She loved to fuck more than any woman—hell, more than any man—I ever met. And good? Bart was right again. Lana was the best.

"What's been happening?" I asked.

"She's been here since one, taking all of us any way we want it," Mike answered.

"Who came in her mouth?" I asked.

Four hands went up, two of them from Andy. "The other hands for Big Jeff," he said sheepishly.

"In the ass?"

"She told us she'd tell our wives if we did her like that," Bill replied.

"Shit. She told us she'd cut us off and that's even worse," Pete snickered.

No anal sex. Period. That was Lana's rule. She'd do anything but that, and if I ever had her ass, she'd never speak to me again.

I saw Bart give Betty a signal. She handed out the beers except for one and brought it to me. I took a swig as Betty's hand slipped under my tee shirt and slid across the top of my jeans. "Let's go somewhere and talk, Ryan," she said seductively.

"No thanks, Betty. I want to join in my wife's gangbang."

"Oh, that's great," someone said and they all begin to talk, like someone had turned on the electricity and a display started. The pressure was off them. I wasn't an angry husband. I was one of the guys participating in fucking the slut.

"I'm going to fuck her ass and you guys are going to help me," I said.

The electricity disconnected. All was quiet again.

"This is what's going to happen. I want her on the bed doggy-style. Mike, you'll hold her head. Pete and Little Jeff will hold her arms. Andy and Bart will hold her legs. I'll plow her from behind. You will hold her like I want her. Understand?"

"Not me," Bart said. "She's too good to give up." Bart didn't know it, but he just bought more trouble than he could handle.

"I'll take the other leg, Ryan. It's the least I can do for you," Jack said.

"That's right, guys. We owe it to Ryan. He's our buddy and he's always been there for us," Mike said. "Let's do it."

Lana was facing the far wall when we entered the bedroom. She was on her hands and knees on the bed with Jeff fucking her doggy-style, driving into her sloppy cunt with all he had. I heard her laugh—a demonic, guttural laugh—like she does when she orgasms. I wondered how many times she had.

Jeff drove hard into her. She pushed back against him and wiggled her hips. "That's it, Baby. Fill me up," she said.

That's what she always said when I came in her.

Mike crawled in front of her with his back against the headboard. Lana thought he wanted his cock sucked and her head dropped into his lap. The others took their places before she realized what was happening.

I pushed Jeff aside and took his place between her legs. His cum drooled out of her, or maybe it was Mike's cum, or whoever's it was. There was a pile of the wet sticky stuff on the sheet under her red and well-used pussy.

"I need a cock in me," she said, raising her head up to look Mike in the face. "Who's next?"

Mike tangled his hands in her hair above the ears on both sides of her face to get a good grip and pulled her head back until his face was near hers. "Ryan," he said.

The world stood still. No one made a sound.

"Ryan? My husband?"

I drove my cock into her loose and well lubed pussy. When I pulled out, there was as much cum on my cock as there was when we fucked at home.

"Yes, Lana. It's me," I said. "Hold still, baby. You're going to love this."

I drove all the way into her ass with one long, hard stroke, burying my cock in her bowels to the hilt. She screamed and started struggling. Lana's strong for her size and her adrenalin pumped, but she was tired from a hard night's fucking and six big guys held her in place. All that twisting and fighting gave my crotch a good massage from her hips and her sphincter spasmed on my cock.

Any other time, all that stimulation would've made me go off like a Roman candle. This time, I wasn't even close. I wanted to do this my way.

She fought until she couldn't move. The guys were holding her up, not holding her still as she sucked in air by the bushels. I took a hip in each hand and slowly began to fuck her ass.

Something happened to her. It must've been the heat, exertion and continual sexual stimulation for a couple of hours. And the hard dick in her asshole, of course. I heard her demonic laugh, but it was different this time, like I'd heard only once before. It was staccato, like she was laughing with the hiccups. Lana was building to a mind-blowing climax.

"Listen," I barked. "Grab her tits, guys. Jack, do her clit. Andy, finger her. Mike, pull her hair. On the beat. Ready. Squeeze. Tug. Tug. Release. Rest. Squeeze. Tug. Tug. Release. Rest."

Betty started clapping the rhythm and chanting the words. The others not doing it chimed in. "Squeeze. Tug. Tug. Release. Rest."

Only Lana and I were off beat. She was twitching, rotating and growling. Her skin were on fire. She cursed and babbled incoherently. The guys holding her were working to keep her in place. The chanting got louder. "Squeeze. Tug. Tug. Release. Rest."

Me? I was driving up her dark hole and struggling to stay in her without cumming. The motions, heat and pressures were excruciating.

"Faster," I said. They picked up the tempo and so did Lana.

I heard her pre-climax laugh. She screeched and yanked herself free. She sat back hard, burying me in her. Her nails dug into my thighs. Her ass tightened on my cock.

It definitely was not fun. The pain was intense, like when you catch your dick in your zipper. I screamed.

Lana screamed, vomited on Mike, and passed out.

Lana stayed there. Betty said she'd take care of her. Pete and Little Jeff took me to the hospital. Dr. Booker was on duty. We all knew Helen, who was three years ahead of us in high school. I showed Helen the puncture wounds made by Lana's claws in my thighs and I showed her my dick.

"Ryan, your penis is horribly bruised. Doesn't it hurt?"

"It's killing me," I replied.

"I'll get some painkiller and an icebag. You can't have sex for a few weeks. Don't even masturbate. If it's not painfree in five days, you need to see me again. I'm going to cleanse and stitch your wounds." She glared at me. "Were these made by a woman?"

"Lana," I replied.

"I've seen wounds made when a woman clawed a man, but none like these. These are wider and deeper." She shook her head in disbelief and started the procedures.

The painkiller wiped me out. I barely remember the guys getting me home and in bed.

Someone shook me. I heard my name being called as I fought to clear the cobwebs from my mind.

"Wake up, Ryan," she said, shaking me again.

"Mom?" I mumbled. "What are you doing here?"

"You're not at home. You're in the hospital and you have been for two days."

Mom look terrified. So did Dad, Mike and Amy who were standing behind her. I turned my head to see Father Morris who looked more terrified and had a crucifix in his hand.

"In the name of the Father, the Son and the Holy Spirit. Amen," Father Morris said as he made the sign of the cross on my forehead.

"What's going on?" I asked.

"Lana's in the hospital, too. She almost died," Mom answered.

"Mike told us what happened at Betty's house. He told us everything," Amy said.

"Lana was possessed by the Devil," Father said. He sounded as scared as he looked. "The anal sex drove him from her body. At least that's what the exorcist thinks. We really don't know."

"They want you to be exorcised," Mom said.

"They want to exorcise all of us there that night," Mike interjected.

"Exorcise the Devil? You're kidding me?"

"The Devil isn't funny, Ryan," Father said piously.

Maybe not, but I snickered anyway. I went to Mass most Sundays and Confession three or four times a year, but I thought demonic possession was bullshit. I didn't say that to Father Morris though. He looked like he had enough problems. They stayed with me and talked for ten minutes or so before Dr. Booker came in.

"Time to leave. He needs his rest," she said. Mom kissed me and they all tottered off. Dr. Booker threw the covers back and checked my thighs. "You're healing more quickly than I expected."

"Good genes," I joked.

"I had the nurse remove the catheter. How's your penis feeling?" she asked. She bent over and took my cock in her hand. "Healing nicely, I see. I think this medicine is what it needs."

She sucked it in her mouth. That surprised me. I always thought of Helen as asexual, even when I was in high school and anything in skirts looked good. I didn't think of her that way as she bobbed on my cock giving me one hell of a good blowjob.

As her hand slowly worked my hard and needy shaft, she looked up at me. I knew that look. It was Lana's look—the one she had when she desperately needed sex.

Or was it the Devil's look?

"The priests are looking for me," Helen said, but it didn't sound like Helen. Her voice was low and guttural. "Don't tell them where I am and you'll have the best sex you ever had."

"I won't tell them," I said.

"That's my good boy," Helen said in that unworldly voice. She lowered her mouth to my cock. In seconds, I spurted my load and she swallowed it. "I'll be back," she said as she left me alone.

Why should I tell the priests? I knew what was happening now. If I managed it, the demon would jump from Helen to another woman when I was ready, so the best sex would be there for me. And I knew how to manage it. I could fuck the Devil away.

The nurse came in. She was a little plump, but that didn't matter. I stared at her. She looked terrified and helpless. A tear rolled down her cheek as she looked at her wedding rings. She shivered, locked the door, and removed her hose and panties.

"Take off everything," I said.

She nodded and undressed before climbing on the bed and impaling herself on my cock. I lay back with my arms behind my head and let her do the work. I was in no hurry. I liked watching her face and her bouncing tits. She humped until she was red-faced and near exhaustion. The room stunk of sex. Her pussy was getting dry and my crotch was soaked in her juices.

She didn't orgasm, but that wasn't important to either of us. Only one thing was important. My orgasm. Clearly, she would fuck herself to death rather than stop before I climaxed.

When I let myself cum, I laughed. It surprised me, and I thought, "Jesus, was that my laugh?"

Guilty Confession.

I'm at the rear bedroom of a lavish condominium watching two guys fuck while a homosexual porn movie plays on the TV.

Henry, the smaller guy on the mattress, is lying on his back with his legs folded against his chest, raising his buttocks. Charles, Henry's spouse, is kneeling between Henry's open thighs, sliding his rigid penis up Henry's buttocks.

"Wow!" Sammy whispers. "That is SO sexy!"

She's a stereotypical bull dyke. Chunky with wide shoulders, a chin and man-short hair, dressed in work boots, blue Dockers, along with a white guy's shirt with its extended sleeves rolled up, but the mix is boy-cute, rather than intimidating.

We're just two hours into a celebration at a wealthy queen's place. The liquor flows freely and individuals slip out to maneuver joints on the rear patio, so everyone is a bit wasted.

Sammy came together with her ultra-femme girlfriend, Fritzie, who's in the living area talking about style with a set of homosexual dress designers. Fritzie's husband would be quite upset to learn that his sexy wife is into butch women and just married him to get his cash.

I'd drifted away from the primary celebration. That's the sex space, using a gay porn movie, condoms and squeeze bottles of lubricant scattered around, so I wasn't surprised to see Charles and Henry nude on the bed getting ready to fuck. I hadn't expected to visit Sammy there watching the guys so intently. I didn't believe butches were into male-male sex.

She turned to look at me. "Enjoying the show?" I asked.

"Oh yeah," she answered. "I've never seen two men ..." She glanced at the TV. "I mean in pornography, but maybe not for real."

Sammy and I were standing side by side at the base of the bed, watching Charles fuck Henry's buttocks while a twink sucked the other's cock on the movie. We were also stealing regular glances at each other. I'd always liked tomboys and she was really sexy with her boyish looks, together with the broad feminine hips extending her Dockers along with the complete breasts satisfying her white top.

She seemed to be enjoying how I looked as well. I'm not handsome, but I am tall, rocky and reasonably athletic, dressed in my normal tight tee-shirt and blue jeans that showed off my huge crotch bulge. It had developed a hell of a lot bigger because I'd walked into the area. And not merely because of Charles, Henry and the movie. Sammy was the main reason behind that growing boner.

"Do you enjoy the series?" Sammy asked.

I nodded. She plastered her entire body on mine and kissed me, hard and open-mouthed with dueling tongues, the way how one homosexual man cries to another.

"Does Fritzie like you kissing her that way," I inquired.

"Not at first." Sammy laughs softly. "But once I get her heated ..." She opened my buttocks and ground her anus on my crotch bulge. "I believe you get the idea."

"I'm definitely getting some thoughts," I stated.

"Can they involve drawing my trousers down and bending me over the mattress?"

"Well, I'd been thinking of a marginally more romantic strategy. However, yeah. Fundamentally, pulling down your pants and bending you over the mattress."

"That is amorous," she said, then kissed me.

Charles and Henry exchanged places on the mattress. Charles got on all fours and faced the TV Henry mounted him from behind and fucked him about.

"I will bend for you," Sammy said. "But the pants stay on. At least for today. Okay?" She bent over, facing the bed and waved her buttocks. It didn't seem like a guy's bum in her tight Dockers, but it was every bit as sexy.

"Sure." I stepped behind her and placed my hands on her buttocks. She ground her ass into my crotch bulge, which made my painfully controlled cock harder. I slip my hands up and fondled her breasts while I humped her crack through our trousers.

On the mattress, Henry is beating Charles. Their groans and slapping sounds of flesh on flesh mingle with the noises from the TV.

"Fuck!" Sammy moaned. "Fuck me!"

"Does that imply trousers down?" I moved my hands back down to her waist and hit her belt.

"Yes." Sammy stiffens and looks about wildly. "But not here where Fritzie could walk in and watch us." She grabbed my hands. "Come with me."

"I'm gonna cum!" Henry gasped, slamming his cock up Charles' buttocks. Sammy hesitates in the bedroom doorway, then goes back and catches a plastic squeeze bottle of lube. She brings me down the hallway to a door that's closed.

She opens the door, pulls me inside and shuts the door. From the dim light through the curtains that are drawn, I could tell it was another bedroom. "I really don't think we're supposed to be here."

"Probably not," Sammy answered. "However, it is personal."

"What if somebody comes in and finds us?"

"You need to fuck or not?"

"Well, as you put it that way." I pull Sammy into my arms and kiss her. She kisses me hard and dirty, much more like a guy than a woman.

Like the rear bedroom, this area has its own bathroom. We go inside, shut the door and flip on the lights. "That's better," I said. "I wish to see you."

"Good." She reaches for the top of her white guy's shirt. "I'd like you to see me."

She undid the buttons from top to bottom in a single smooth movement. "All of me."

She pulled her top open, displaying her medium-sized breasts. She isn't wearing a bra. Her big nipples have been put in wide areolas.

"You like that?" she said, arching her back and thrusting her breasts while she removed her top and put it on the counter. "Am I sexy as a boy?"

"You sure are." I strip my tee-shirt off and drop it onto Sammy's top. "Naked chests are sexy anyhow. Yours is outstanding." I inspect her breasts. They fit her body perfectly. "But don't take my word for this." I pointed down at the huge bulge in my jeans.

She smiles. "It is kinda simple to inform men." She took her shoes and socks off, followed with her Dockers, leaving her nude except for tight-fitting boyshorts. "Women's pussies get wet and our nipples get hard, but that isn't so evident."

"Obvious enough." I kiss her firmly on the lips then proceed down to her buttocks. I licked her flesh and sucked on her nipples, making them swell between her compressed lips.

Sammy moaned gently and reached down to stroke my rigid pole through my extended blue jeans. "My nipples are a lot tougher now. And my pussy's wet, too." She grabbed my hands and put it between her thighs. The crotch of her boyshorts remained moist. Not moist. Wet. "Do you feel it?"

"Oh yeah!" Somehow, my penis, cruelly trapped in my panties got harder.

"You are nevertheless half-dressed," Sammy said. "I'm nearly nude" She unfastens my belt and opened my fly. I've gone commando along with my suddenly-freed cock.

"Oh my!" She bent her hands around my rigid rod. "I guess we're even now."

"Yeah." I press my hands against Sammy's crotch and crook my middle finger, running it up and down the moist fabric covering her slit. "Half dressed and playing with each others' crap."

"We might be dressed." Sammy guides my hands on her boyshorts' waistband. I pull them down. She rips them away. "Like this." She pulled down my jeans. I finish off them. Afterward, we adopt. Naked.

"You know how to handle a girl," Sammy purrs. "Perhaps you've had lots of?"

"No. Just a few." I'd lost my virginity to a woman my age. Obviously, she'd been a tomboy and was a competitive one. Luckily, we'd used condoms. My next girl was a married woman in her mid-20s, with a long-haul trucker husband, two children, along with an insatiable sex drive. She taught me nearly everything I know about sex with girls.

"Well, you're still ahead of me." For the very first time, Sammy seemed nervous. "I've never been with a boy. I mean, feeling and kissing, sure. Along with a few hand tasks and stuff. However, I don't let some of them set their dick in me."

"What would you like to do?" I asked. We'd both been drinking and decreasing our inhibitions. "A quickie at a toilet where someone can walk in and grab us is not the perfect means to give your virginity."

"Perhaps it's not ideal. But, you're the guy I want. And I'd like you now, so this is the ideal time and place."

"We can organize another time. I've got a great apartment. Private. Wine, candlelight, soft music—"

"I'm ready now." Sammy dropped to her knees and carried my rigid dick in her mouth.

Sammy was a great cocksucker. She stroked my rigid shaft and fondled my balls while hammering her lips round my corneal ring, swirling her tongue on my cock-head.

"Oh yeah." I ran my fingers through her hair. "That's really great."

She allowed my dick to slide from her mouth. "It gets better." She slides her hands up my shaft and grasped my flaring cock-head between her thumb and index finger, then kissed and licked my balls. Eventually, she chose a ball and then put another into her mouth and lashed at them with her tongue.

Sammy enabled my balls come and go back, and went back to my cock. She took it all in her mouth and bobbed on the swollen shaft and head. I slowly rolled up my butt. She stroked and sucked my stiff pole with stylish motions.

I moved quicker. Shortly, I'm fucking her, driving in and out of her mouth while holding the back of her head. Girls aren't supposed to enjoy that, but it's getting Sammy more excited.

The pressure in my balls is attaining to a boiling point. I pulled my throbbing cock from her mouth before I burst.

"This was fun." Sammy stood up and kissed me passionately. Subsequently, she bent over the counter and stuck her shapely buttocks out. She grinned at me in the mirror. "Now, fuck me. I really don't wish to be gone too long. Fritzie will wonder where I am."

I measure up supporting Sammy. "You attracted the warmth, but no condoms. Does that mean?"

"Yeah." Sandy reaches back and pulls her buttocks wide open, showing me her small pink puckered hole. "Fuck my butt. I would like to feel you come inside me."

"Okay." I lubricate my index finger and pressed the tip to Sammy's asshole. She purred and arched her back. I pushed my finger ahead. It slid in easily, all the way to my curly-haired knuckles. I pushed it in and out a couple of times, then yanked it out, added more lube and stuck it back in.

"Come," Sammy said. "I'm ready. I haven't had a real cock inside me, but there were dildos."

I smeared lube in my rigid prick. "I really wish we had more time ..."

"This is the best first time for me personally," Sammy said. "I enjoy the danger. I know that's odd, however ... Never mind. Just fuck me. Fuck my ass. Now!"

I push my cock-head to the middle of her puckered hole. She yelled as I stretched her anal muscles. "You Ok?" I asked.

"Sure." She rocked back, forcing my cock-head through her anal ring and into her depths. "Now fuck me. Fuck me like I'm a guy."

"Taking a dick up your bum is butch as hell." I drew back and then pushed ahead.

"Cum in me." Sammy braced a hand on the counter, then slid the opposite hand between her thighs. "Fuck me hard!"

"All right." I grip Sammy's waist and pound her buttocks, pulling almost out and then driving home, which made a loud slapping sound as my elbows slammed into her buttocks.

"Oh fuck yeah!" Sammy gasps, fingering her pussy frantically. "Hammer my bum."

The cum boiling in my nuts is approaching to the exploding point. "I'm getting close ..."

"Oh yeah," Sammy said. "Give me your large, hot load," she yelled as I hit her ass, pumping a tough, sexy jet into her depths. She kept crying, cumming over and over because I pounded her ass.

We eventually finished. Sammy and I temporarily cuddled, then got cleaned up, dressed, then rejoin the party. Fritzie was still speaking to the trend queens. She hadn't missed Sammy. From the rear bedroom, three brand new guys are on the mattress. The center one is fucking the front person's buttocks while the previous person butt fucks the center guy. I watched for some time, then wandered away.

It's time to hit the street. I've had a fantastic afternoon. Sammy and I've got each other's telephone numbers, too, so that's always a good bonus.

The Family Gangbang

My son Daniel and I stood next to each other, nude and stroking our hard throbbing cocks as we watched the erotic scene unfolding in front of us. My mother Helen was on her back on the bed with her legs in the air, stretched as wide as humanly possible, with my father Robert tonguing his wife's cunt on his knees for everything he'd been worth. It was Friday evening and, as always, my parents travelled with my family to Roma for our yearly vacation, hopefully they will stay for the weekend before leaving us to go back, arriving less than an hour ago and no time wasted in getting down to business. Keep in mind that since my mom, son and I were nude when they came-we rarely wear clothes in our hotel suite privacy unless the room service phones-it would have been trying not to.

"Bloody hell," my wife Sandra said, coming into the room with a plate of sandwiches from the hotels kitchen and wearing only her beautiful smile, "didn't take long for those two to get going." "You know what granny and granpas are like," Daniel said, laughing at his mother and firing his dick again, "they're... what's the word?" "Insatiable," I said, pounding my own excited prick in my hands while I stared at the gorgeous pair. With each twitch of dad's tongue, Mum's whimperings kept rising and dropping, and as he reached her clit and started to nibble at it, the whimperings turned to long grunts of fulfilmenst, with high volume that could raise the dead.

"Alright," said my wife, putting the plate of burgers, cheese and pickle if I wasn't mistaken, on the table and turning over toward us, exposing Daniel and I to a full frontal mouth watering view of her succulent boobs and juicy cunt, "looks like these need some love," she added, referring to mine and our son's cocks with her shaking her head. It wouldn't have been the first time that day, before my son and I left for work, Sandra, Daniel and I had shared another of our mind-blowing threesomes in the morning, but the two of us loved it so much we weren't about to say no as Sandra fell to her knees before us.

"Sure fucking do, mom," responded Daniel, his cock as firm as mine as the rock of ages, "I'm starving for a blowjob." "Everybody would think you have not had one for ages, "Sandra giggled, taking a dick on each hand and enjoying the sight of showing her our two fat rods, each just an inch away from her admiring gaze, "it was only this morning that I woke you up with one." Daniel had proven himself to be a swift learner in the short space of time following his initiation session, both Sandra and I were immensely proud of him and his huge ass, and he was now a very accomplished sexualist, expert at licking pussy and sucking cock as well as giving and receiving cum, making the long wait for him to join us all worthwhile.

I stood back and started masturbating while Sandra, without a word, quickly pulled the stupendous dick of our son into her hand, gagging the hard pole as it reached her throat back. Daniel grinned happily as the very accomplished mouth of his mother wrapped around his incredible youthful manhood, the shaft disappeared entirely inside until Daniel's equally impressive balls slammed against her jaw. It was a fantastic sight, my wife sucking our son as my parents went to bed to do their business. I shifted to a spot where, from a single point of view, I could see all the action, never letting my dick go for a moment, realizing that my turn would come soon. There's no envy at all in our gangbangs, we're a loving family that looks after each other earnestly and looks after everybody's needs and I was able to be a voyeur for the next few moments as the atmosphere in the bedroom was pungent with the heady aroma of spicy tabou sex.

"that is correct," I told Sandra, "our boy's dick Is here please do justice by sucking." Sandra certainly didn't need any motivation, she was undeniably one of the world's greatest cocksuckers, a fact that proved beyond doubt as Daniel rocked back and forth on his strong muscular thighs, his cute sexy bare arse cheeks quivering and his head thrown back into ecstasy. Sandra enjoyed sucking cock so she went to town with all the powers she had in her hands-and they were and are tremendous powers too - and it was awesome to see Daniel is so sweet, happy and pleased to be part of our family gang bangs now. Mom backed off her father's head on the bed softly and maneuvered until she was on her bended knees, her elbows resting on her duvet and her bottom lying on the pillows. Dad stood up and grinned at me, his eyes falling to my dick before turning his attention to Sandra and Daniel who had been lost on the other side of the room in a world of theirs.

"Come and show your mother how much you love her, Peter," my father said, "when I go and have some fun with that sexy wife of yours." Dad moved across the house, giving my cock and balls a fast sensation as he did, his own dick absolutely on the horn, then I went over to my girlfriend, my mouth Brushing openly at the sight of her pink arse hole, without any trace of shame or guilt. "You're going to fuck me, son?" asked my mother, breathing huskily over her shoulder and laughing at me, licking her lips at the sight of my pulsating cock. "In a minute, mum," I said, "I would like to feel that hot juicy pussy first." "Get it over with then, sweetheart," mum said, "my cunt just deserves a good lick and fuck." I crawled to the bed and buried my mouth just mum's arse, rubbing my tongue up and down her butt and then rolled over and placed myself until I was on my back with my face between her spread legs. Looking up, I had the most beautiful glimpse of her maternal pussy and for fear that the anticipation would make me cum my load so soon I had to let go of my dick.

Gently I grabbed mum's ass and pulled her against me, then I stuck my tongue and started to taste my birthplace again, her cunt dripping with dad's spit, determined to show to mum being a good pussy licker like my dad is hereditary. I cant put a figure again on the numbers of time I have done cunnilingus on my own mother but I never tiro of it, I love to lick her vagina and savor her pussy juice.

I heard soft groans coming from Sandra across the room as she let Daniel's cock slip off her ass, replacing it directly with her father-in-law's. Daniel, He was satisfied with the blowjob he got, and went to bed to see his father's pussy more closely. My father groaned as his daughter in-law showed her wily charms to him, showing his penis the same attention to detail that Daniel's had.

"Don't stand there alone, Daniel," my mother gasped as my tongue found her stimulated clit and I began to circle her, "let your old granny suck your cock." "Go, gran," Daniel responded, "you're not old, you're young." "That's it," my father said, his hands on his hips, laughing with paternal satisfaction while watching the action on the bed as Sandra continued to enjoy it. Daniel didn't waste a second as he turned around and stood in front of his grandma for the second sucking of his dick that night and I heard him groan happily as my mother wrapped her lips around his pride and joy. An overwhelming sense of pride ran through me in my family, particularly for my mum. I'm not going to give up her generation, let's just say she's not in the first blossom of a teenager, but she's really looked after herself, like my father, and neither of them looks anywhere near their exact ages, and mom, mainly, is still as beautiful and sexy as she was when I was first allowed to join her and dad all those years ago-and we had a really sensational threeso baby.

After ten minutes I agreed that enough was enough when it came to the pussy licking, all mum wanted was a decent fucking now. She was still sucking Daniel with satisfaction when I slipped out from under her thighs and got in a standing position, realizing that dad and Sandra had also changed positions and were sitting on the couch, perched sixty-nine style each other. Dad made a real meal from the cunt of my mom, and Sandra again demonstrated her sucking and licking abilities, now buried deep in her mouth with the balls of her father-in-law.

"Come on, sweetheart," my mother said, "do not keep me waiting for a moment longer." "Your wish is my order, mum," I responded, lubbing up my cock and rubbing mum's cunt with some baby oil afterwards. Daniel turned around to watch me screw his gran and he didn't have to wait long, I reached in and deftly stuck my incestuous dick into mum's vagina, a position he had the great privilege of knowing several times before now, though every time he feels like the first one. Daniel was closely watching the scene, his own cock so hard it was pointing directly to the ceiling that if it was a compass I could have found my way north by it. He had his foreskin peeled back and the pink glossy head of his dick glowed in the lamplight, my mouth watering as I looked up the cock of my son while concurrently fucking my mother and making a mental note at the back of my mind to give Daniel a nice long parental blowjob and more before our new family gangbang finished.

Outside, a loud thunder rumble led to the sound of our sex party, accompanied by a flash of lightning that illuminated the bedroom like a firework display. Then the rain came down, hammering in stair-rods on the roof to cool the air of its extreme summer heat and make space a cosy sanctuary of sensual ambient light, perfect for a cozy family sex party. I pounded my dick in and out of mum's cunt as the rain continued to fall, her grunts of ecstasy grew louder as she pulled back to meet every stroke, bringing one leg up on the bed to allow Daniel a better view as he dropped to his knees, wavering his cock with one fist, and fondling my balls with the other.

"That's right," my son replied, "fuck mum dur, she likes it." " I'm sure, "my mother succeeded in expressing between grunting and groaning," don't stop I love it, you're doing an excellent job. "Go on, boy," I heard my father tell, briefly relinquishing his tongue from Sandra's cunt to speak, "you know what an old slut your mother's." "God, I love being called a whore," mum giggled at a prostitute.

"We're all sluts here, mom," I've managed to say in between my intense concentration to give her as much satisfaction as I can muster.

"Sure they're fucking," Daniel giggled, bending between my thighs and sticking out his tongue, kissing my balls as my cock kept teasing my mum. The tongue of my son felt so good on my nutsack that I knew it wasn't going to be long before I filled the cunt of mum and, sure enough, a few seconds later, I groaned as I erupted my cum deeply in her. Mum twisted as she felt my spunk burning in her intestines, and Daniel stood up, whooping with satisfaction and rubbing his dick through the air, my father let out serious moaning as he exploded in his mom's mouth.

My father rolled back on the mattress, gasping for breath as he tried to regain equilibrium while mum's vagina dripped my cum over the bedsheets. Sandra still had a mouthful of the spunk of my dad, and savored every drop and drank as much of it as she could. Daniel stepped over and softly clasped Sandra by the hands and turned her back until she was on her bottom, then knelt before her and began to run Slowly his tongue was sticked along the groove between his mother's smooth, silky cunt lips.

"That's the way, baby," I said, pounding on my erect shaft, "using your tongue like your gramps and I taught you. Lick that pussy well." Daniel was in ecstasy when he demonstrated his love for his mother with a great long lick from his own home. While my son began to lick with a skill that belied his tender years, he reached with one hand to grope the luscious boobs of Sandra while at the same time wavering his hard cock with the other, his body functioning as a clockwork as mother and son grew to an even higher horniness level.

"Damn, that looks really good," my father said, following his previous ejaculation in Sandra's mouth, whose cock was now rock hard again.

Dad saying the F word must have been recognized in Daniel's brain because he suddenly stopped licking Sandra's cunt and grinned at his mother as he grabbed her by Her arms folded around her, and placed her on her hands and knees. "Here, boy," I said, giving Daniel the lube, "just use that."

Despite the fact that Sandra's cunt was now completely lubricated with Daniel's saliva, his cock still had to be greased and he lubbed himself quickly and smeared some into his mother to help his dick on his way. Instead he bent over her and put his fantastic manhood into Sandra's cunt while his father moved over and crawled to the bed with his wife, both of them resting in each other's arms while they watched their grandson fuck their daughter-in-law.

"Your lad is a right chip off the old block, boy," said my father, a comment that mum nodded in approval with her ear. My parents had an unimpeded view of my bare arse with my back to them and I could feel their eyes boring into it, knowing that both of them would want to fuck my ass when they were fully healed from the first round of sex in the evening, mum with her silicone dick and dad with his real one.

"You must be very proud of him," my mother said as I saw the exquisite bare bottom of my son rising and falling as he thrusted my wife in and out. Daniel's arse cheeks were silky smooth, firm, and round as should be a male arse, complemented by his crack's sexy long slit.

Daniel frequently went to the gym to keep himself in condition and all the hard work has paid off handsomely and his firm sexy buttocks have been and are a visual pleasure. As if conscious that I was ogling his ass, Daniel reached out his hands and clasped his buns, pulling them apart and spreading them wide to reveal his ruby red rosebud that twitched with anticipation and I licked my lips at the sight of the long thin sexy lines that emerged on the walls of his arse as he moved in and out of his anal muscles, pointing his hole at me.

Instead I turned my head back to watch the scene before me; I couldn't contain my lust any longer so I knelt down behind Daniel and began to cover his arse cheeks with lots of sweet little kisses as he continued pumping in and out of Sandra, giving her the first fuck of the evening and one she will recall for a very long time.

Daniel's butt was so tempting that I stopped kissing his cheeks and started licking away to my heart's content at his smooth sweet arsehole, even though his cheeks bobbled around making it challenging to rimm a tad as he fucked my mom, the three of us, mum, dad and son joined together. Mum and dad were on the sidelines yelling and cheering encouragemtnt as they listened and it turned us all on even more to learn that we had such an excited crowd.

Finally I had to come up for air and Sandra and Daniel took the opportunity to change position with Daniel parking his arse on the floor and Sandra dropping herself onto him, gasping her talented pussy onto the equally talented fucking pole of our friend. Sandra's eyes were closed tightly while her vagina slowly swallowed up every inch of Daniel's cock-and he had about seven inches in all-while Daniel, always considerate to the desires of his mother, waited patiently until she was as comfortable as possible and ready for him to continue the fuck in earnest.

Sandra's grunts of satisfaction were even louder than mum's, as Daniel poked and prodded her with all the passion and excitement that he had acquired from our sex sessions in just a few months, showing yet again that he was no longer the gangly teenager of yesteryear but a guy who had matured spectacularly into adulthood. Any parent should take pride in having a son like Daniel.

"Fuck me, sweetheart," Sandra whispered, "give me it fast." Once this evening I fired my load, I was as horny again as I was watching my wife fuck my son. Throughout the trial, Sandra's eyes had remained rigidly closed, but now she opened them and grinned, pleased to have such an attentive audience, and spread her legs as wide as possible to allow me and her parents-in-law the best view of the forbidden penetration. There was a twinkle in Sandra's eyes and I knew what she wanted; as Daniel continued pounding the strong greasy quim of his mother with his all-conquering power tool, I stepped forward as Sandra opened her mouth and slipped into her mouth as I pushed my dick.

This is one of Sandra's favorite positions, both sucking and being fucked while she, Daniel and I enjoy our regular daily threesomes but the fact that my parents were with us for the weekend and enjoying and watching made it even more fun. The cheese and pickle sandwiches that Sandra had so carefully prepared earlierlay sadly forgotten where she had put them on the bed. As indeed was the rain that came outside still

Yet mum and dad were no longer able to just sit and watch there. A sudden movement behind me and a snap of the bed springs and my parents rolled over to join us, our naked bodies squeezed together in a sweaty group of fuckers from school. Mum dropped to her knees behind me and began to lick my arse crack as dad bent in and kissed me hard on his lips, both of us snaking our tongues into each other's mouths; Seconds later, when Daniel rose up to insert his semen deep into his mother's cunt, he let out a prolonged groan.

"Oh yeah, boy!" Sandra yelled, relinquishing my dick from her mouth while her son filled her cunt with his precious incestuous spunk, "you made me proud again." "My pleasure, mum," Daniel answered as Sandra hauled herself off her prick and started fingering her pussy, catching some of Daniel's spunk on her fingertips, then Holding them in her mouth to lick them out while Daniel's fingertips turned. Sandra collapsed into his arms and as a dad they kissed passionately on his lips, and I broke the kiss and he fell to his knees and quickly took my dick into his mouth, sucking on the stiff pole long and hard.

Mum was still kissing my arse so I bent slightly over, reached round with my hands and opened my buns to allow her tongue better access; now mum wasn't just running her hot wet tongue up and down my crack but giving me the full rimjob, her tongue testing my ass as if for the first time and still feeling just as thrilling as when she first gave my arsehole.

 "Look at gran and gramps having fun with dad," said Daniel, while sitting around Sandra with his neck, brushing her boobs with his fingertips, and my wife grinned at us wisely. Mum made a real arsehole meal with her beautiful tongue and dad sucked greedy on my dick as if it were a brand new sight for him.

"I think," Sandra said, "it's my turn to give back the compliment. Helen, where did you put that dildo of yours?" "In my bag over there," my mom replied, quickly returning her interest to my bum after speaking.

Sandra reached inside the pack, taking the strap-on out and wrapping it around her neck. "Come now, my man," she said to Daniel, "go to bed and hang your arse in the rain." Daniel did as he was biding; his magnificent arse looked even more incredible hanging in the atmosphere. He didn't have to be asked what to do, he picked his buttocks and opened them wide, his gaping arsehole on display to every single member of his family. Sandra lubbed her dick with the oil and smeared a few in Daniel's mouth, then reached in and slipped into Daniel's ass, sweet and gentle at first, giving our son time to acclimatize to the experience, then as he relaxed Sandra upped the pace, her strap-on paving the way for Daniel to take some real live cocks before we went to sleep, with my father and me.

"For now, I think it's pretty rimming," my father said to my mum, letting my cock slip out of his ass, "I thanked our son right his earlier efforts." Mum pulled her tongue from my arsehole and patted my cheeks. "I hope it has lubricated pretty well by now," she said. "Why don't you get on the bed next to Daniel, baby," Mum said to me, "when I get my phone, I have need to get some snaps of this for our set of pornography." Daniel's grunts and groans grew louder by the minute with every inch of Sandra's strap-on he took. I climbed up beside him to the bed and got in the same position, sticking my bum out to my parents as mum fumbled in the camera bag. Dad lubbed me dry, and then himself, and his cock went in like a dream, as always in the past. How the bed hasn't shrunk under Daniel's combined weight and how I get fucked, by my father's mother and me, I'll never know.

"It looks fantastic," said Mum, rubbing her cunt before approaching the camera, "now," she went on, in the strident tones it meant she wasn't to be played with as her family fucked around her, "how about some nice new album snaps? Smile, yes!"

MILF Sex in Public with a Stranger

My name is Paula and I am Sunday school teacher at my local church. I am 45 years old and I've been in a ho-hum marriage for 25 years. My husband is very bland and boring and doesn't believe in trying new and exciting things in bed. I never thought in a million years that I'd be the type of woman to have sex with a stranger -let alone in a public place! But, I've been sexually-starved for years. When a hot, young stranger showed interest in me, I just couldn't help myself!

My name is Paula Weathers—well, it's been Paula Weathers for the past 25 years, anyway. My maiden name was actually Paula Garrett before I married my husband, Jacob Weathers. My husband and I live in a quaint little 3-bedroom house in our small southern town. We raised two boys who are both now off in college. I am very proud of both of them, though I do miss them being home, sometimes. My husband works a lot and I have been a stay-at-home mother since Day 1. I am also a Sunday school teacher at our local church and I lead a women's Bible study group every Wednesday evening.

On Tuesday evenings, I like to sit on a bench at the local park and prepare for the following day's Bible study lesson. One day, while doing just that, a group of young local college boys pulled up into the parking lot near the bench where I was sitting.

Living in a small town as long as I have been, I usually recognize many of the local young men and women; however, I did not recognize anyone in this particular group of young people. There were 3 young men and 2 young women, who all looked to be around 19 or 20 years old.

The young women got out of the car first. One of them was tall and thin with long, curly hair and a beautiful face. She was so pretty she could have easily been a model. The other girl got out next. She was shorter than the first girl, and she had short, wavy hair and a perfect set of plump, pursed lips. Looking at those pretty young girls made me think of how hot I once was, about 20 years ago. I bit my lip with envy as I watched the young college girls in their short, tight summer shorts and tank tops, with their perfect hour-glass figures, hurrying over toward the basketball court while giggling back and forth to each other.

Two of the young guys got out of the car next. Both of the young men were tall and handsome, with chiseled faces and muscular, toned bodies. Their skin glistened in the fading sunlight as they also began to make their way toward the basketball court.

Ahh, to be young and beautiful again, I thought to myself. Not that I felt particularly old or ugly, but back when we were young, my husband and I used to be so hot for one another. He used to make me feel sexy and gorgeous, like I was the only woman in the world. Lately, however, he barely pays me any attention at all. We barely touch anymore, let alone kiss or fuck. He used to ravage my body in every room of our house, but somewhere along the way, he seemed to lose interest in sex—or maybe he'd just lost interest in me.

I've tried to throw myself into the Word and focus on Bible study and Sunday school, but the yearning in my loins only seems to increase with every passing day. It has literally been years since my husband and I have had sex, and I feel sexually starved on a daily basis. When the third young man got out of the car, I realized exactly how much I was longing for some sexual satisfaction.

The third young man was tall and gorgeous, just like his peers, but there was something else about him that caught my eye. While the other two boys were wearing tee shirts and athletic shorts, this young man was wearing a form-fitting tank top and a pair of thin, dark-colored shorts that swayed in the gentle breeze as he strolled casually across the park grass.

He was absolutely breath-taking! His short, shiny hair was pulled back away from his chiseled face and his arms and upper body were so muscular and hard-looking, I couldn't help but stare. I didn't even notice how hard I was staring at the gorgeous young hunk until he turned his head and looked at me, flashing me an open-mouth smile as he made his way over toward the basketball court, where his friends were already gathered.

I gasped in surprise at his sexy smile. Almost unconsciously, I flashed a smile right back at him. I almost couldn't believe he'd actually noticed me. Usually, no one really bothers to look my way when I'm sitting on the park bench, looking through my Bible—especially not a hot young hunk like him! My heart instantly began to beat a little faster when I realized he'd actually smiled when he'd caught me staring at him.

I quickly lowered my head to look back down at my Bible, feeling slightly nervous for reasons I couldn't quite put my finger on. I almost felt like a young girl with an instant crush. It was just a smile, I thought to myself. What am I getting so worked up about?

I turned the page of my Bible and pretended to go back to reading it, but a part of me still felt as if the young, handsome man's eyes were still on me. What am I thinking? There's no way a young jock like him would be interested in me! I tried to go back to concentrating on my Bible reading, but the feeling that he was still watching just wouldn't go away.

I knew that I wasn't a pig or anything. In fact, I had managed to keep a nice figure over the years, and my hair was still long and full with plenty of bounce left in it. I didn't have the crow's feet around my eyes that most people over 35 seem to develop as they age, and my breasts were actually still pretty perky for my age, as well. My ass, though not as tight as it once was back in my twenties, was still quite nice, which often made me wonder why my husband seemed so distant, lately. I had put so much effort into keeping myself up for him over the years, that it really hurt that he seemed completely uninterested in me anymore.

Just then, a deep, husky voice from behind me jolted me out of my thoughts.

"Hey there! Whatcha reading?" the voice asked, startling me from my silent reflections. I looked up with a start, surprised to see that the hunky young man who had smiled at me was now standing right next to the bench I was sitting on.

"Uh…um…Thessalonians?" I stuttered back, nervously. He had caught me completely off guard and I was stammering away like an anxious young child.

"Was that a statement or a question?" he asked, looking down at me with a coy grin. If hadn't known any better, I would've thought he was flirting with me. Good thing I knew better.

"I-I'm sorry, it's just that…you startled me," I replied, feeling both shaky and excited.

"Hmm. I startle you and you apologize to me. Wow, sounds kind of backwards, doesn't it?" The handsome young man chuckled lightly at his own statement. His smile lit up his entire face. I was instantly smitten.

I smiled back up at him.

"I'm Paula," I said, feeling the blush that I knew was filling up both of my cheeks. I extended my hand toward the spirited young man.

"Doug," he replied, and gave my hand a firm, yet friendly shake. "Mind if I join you for a bit?"

"Not at all," I replied, almost unconsciously, scooting over on the bench to make room for him to sit down.

"Are you a local?" he asked, sitting down beside me.

"Yes, I am. Born and raised," I answered.

"Yeah, I'm from the city, myself. I'm out here visiting family. It's a bit too quiet around here for me, though. I don't think I could live here. I'd get bored." He looked directly into my eyes. "Unless, of course, I had someone as beautiful and sexy as you to occupy my time."

Did he just call me sexy? I thought to myself. My mind was in a haze. I knew I was blushing, but I couldn't help it. I also couldn't stop smiling. Without even consciously thinking about it, I covered my left hand with my right, attempting to hide my wedding band.

"It doesn't bother me that you're married, Paula," Doug said bluntly, glancing down at my hands.

"It-it doesn't?" I asked, inquisitively. Somehow, though, I wasn't really surprised.

"Nope, not one bit." He took my hand in his and lifted it up to his lips. He kissed the top of my hand and I immediately felt a jolt of electricity race through my entire body when his soft, smooth lips touched my skin.

"Mind if we go somewhere a little bit more…private?" Doug asked me, raising a perfectly-groomed eyebrow at me.

"What did you have in mind?" I asked him, completely forgetting about the open Bible that was still sitting on my lap.

"There's a nice little spot under the bridge, not too far from here," he replied. "We could watch the rest of the sunset. I hear it looks beautiful from there."

I was totally lost in his eyes. They were so beautiful and so full of life. I don't know why or how, but I also saw desire in the gorgeous young guy's eyes. It sent a shiver down my spine that hadn't felt in years. He was looking at me the way my husband used to, but hadn't in a very long time. It ignited something in me that I hadn't even realized was still there. I wanted this young man and I wanted him badly.

I watched his eyes glance down at my breasts. I was wearing a conservative-style blouse that was tight-fitting and hugged my bosom nicely, though it didn't show off any cleavage. His eyes traveled back up to my face.

"Shall we?" he asked, holding out his arm.

"Sure, why not?" I affirmed and closed the Bible on my lap, setting it down on the bench.

Doug and I walked arm-in-arm across the park as the sun was just beginning to set. He told me about his home back in the city and the University he attended, where he was studying journalism.

In a few moments, we had reached the underpass just beneath the bridge. It was almost completely deserted, as the last of the park-goers were clearing out for the evening. As soon as we were completely beneath the underpass, Doug wasted no time making his move on me.

He pushed me up against the wall of the underpass and kissed me on my mouth, hard and passionately, the way my husband used to, back when we were younger.

"God, you're so fucking hot," he whispered, breaking away from our kiss to look at me. It was then that I realized I was actually his fantasy. I was something he wanted more than anything else at that moment, and it turned me on more than I could even imagine.

His lips came down on mine again, and his tongue slid between my lips. He explored my mouth with it, moaning and breathing hard as his hands found my breasts and cupped and squeezed them through the thin fabric of my blouse. I was instantly wet between my thighs. I was moaning and breathing just as hard as he was. I hadn't felt so aroused in a very long time.

He began to unbutton my blouse as we kissed like two horny teenagers. Our mouths intertwined as we sucked each other's tongues and gently bit each other's lips. Every time his tongue touched mine, I felt a twinge between my legs, and I knew my pussy was getting wetter for him by the minute.

He opened up my blouse and quickly pushed my bra up to reveal my soft, large breasts. My nipples were already rock-hard from his touch and I moaned deeply when his took them into his strong, warm hands.

"God, your tits are so fucking nice!" he whispered, his voice raspy with desire. He lowered his head down and took my left breast into his mouth. His tongue felt so good against my nipple as he licked around and around in a circular motion and then gently bit down, causing a light yelp to escape my lips.

"Oh, yes! Yes, Doug, yes!" I whispered, wanting more and more of his touches and kisses. My flesh was on fire for him. He took my other breast in his mouth, holding it steady with his hands and teasing the nipple with his tongue. I felt another twinge between my legs as I felt his cock hardening against my thigh, through the fabric of his shorts.

He slid his hand down my torso and hurriedly raised my thin skirt up until it was bunched up on my hips. I was on fire for him and only he could put it out. He slid his hand between my legs, rubbing my clit through my silk panties. I was so fucking turned on, I could have cum right then, but I wanted to really explode on this young man's cock, so I forced myself to hold back. It took all of my willpower not cream in right there in my panties.

He rubbed and stroked my clit through my panties, causing me to hiss and moan and grind against his fingers.

"Oh, oh, yes, yes…" I couldn't stop saying "yes" to him. I wanted to cry out "more," but "yes" is what kept coming out of mouth between moans, groans, deep breaths and heated pants of pleasure.

"I want to taste this pussy," he moaned into my ear, as he nibbled on it, sticking his tongue inside of it and sucking on my earlobe. His other hand was massaging and squeezing my right breasts as his thumb played with my fully-erect nipples. I was already in ecstasy, but I wanted even more of him.

He slid my panties down and kneeled down between my legs, pushing my right one to the side, slightly, to make more room for his head. And then I felt him, his tongue and his lips, soft and warm against the folds of my cunt. It was already hot and wet for him.

He moaned as he sucked my clit into his mouth and started flicking his tongue against it, hungrily. Again, I wanted to cum so badly. I could have cum, instantly, right there on his beautiful lips, but again, I forced myself with everything in me to hold it back. I writhed in ecstasy, grinding my pussy lips onto his face and moaning and panting in pleasure.

 "Oh God! Yes!" I cried out, grabbing his head and running my finger through his thick, shiny hair, pushing his head forward, further onto me. His lips and tongue felt so good against my pussy, I knew I couldn't take much more or I was gonna squirt my cum all over his handsome face.

 "Ahh, you're gonna make me cum, baby!" I warned, holding his head in my hands and looking down at him with a drunken look of passion on my face.

 "You're not allowed to cum yet," he told me, his voice muffled against my crotch. "You're gonna cum on this cock. And, I'm gonna make you cum like you've never cum before."

I moaned from the sound of his words. They sounded so good to me and I felt yet another twinge between my legs at the sound of them. It had been so long since anyone had made me feel this way. So beautiful, so sexy and so "wanted."

He wanted me. He wanted to fuck me, and he wanted to fuck me like he'd never fucked anyone else before. And I wanted him to fuck me, too. I wanted to feel his long, thick, hard cock buried deep down inside of my hot, wet pussy. I wanted to squirt my cum juice all over his dick and feel his hot cum deep inside of me.

He rose up from his knees, slid his shorts down and pulled out his thick, rock-hard cock. It looked so good to me! I wanted to taste it, suck it down deep into depths of my throat and give him some the same sexual pleasure he had just been giving me.

I took his cock into my hands, stroking it and rubbing it, feeling throb inside of my hands. It turned me on to feel this young, vibrant, handsome man's cock throbbing with desire for me. Me, a middle-aged housewife who days of being young and vibrant were all but long gone. But, not in his eyes. In his eyes, I was the sexiest, most amazing older woman in the world, right now. I was his "MILF", and I was loving every minute of it.

This time I forced him up against the wall of the underpass and dropped down to my knees. I didn't care about the hard ground beneath them, I just wanted to feel Doug's cock in my mouth and hear him writhe and moan from the pleasure I planned to give him. I was a well-seasoned cock-sucker, it had just been such a long time since I'd gotten the chance to put my oral skills to use. I couldn't wait to taste him.

I held his hard, throbbing cock in my hands and placed the tip of it up to my lips. I looked up and saw his beautiful eyes staring down at me with overwhelming desire in them. It turned me on to no end. With a coy smirk on my face, I licked the head of his cock with my tongue, causing a hiss of pleasure to escape his lips.

"Suck it, Paula. Suck this cock," he told me, his voice barely above a raspy, passion-filled whisper. He didn't have to tell me twice. I slid the head of his dick into my mouth, opening wide and running my tongue over the head. He gasped and grabbed my head.

"Ahh, yesss..." he hissed. "Fuuuck..."

He closed his eyes, threw his head back and began to thrust his hips with the rhythm of my sucking. I took his cock deep down into to my mouth, moaning with passion as I did so. He tasted so good! I could feel his pre-cum leaking out of the head of his cock and I licked it with my tongue, tasting the sweet, salty thickness of it.

"Mmm," I said, my voice muffled by his hard, throbbing cock filling my mouth. I sped up my pace, sucking long and hard, holding on to his hips for balance. He grabbed my hair and wrapped his hands in it, pushing my mouth down further onto his dick.

"Ah, ah, ah, yesss! Shit! Fuck!" he muttered, between grunts and groans of pleasure. "You suck it so fucking good, Paula!"

If my mouth hadn't been completely filled with his cock, I would've smiled up at him. Instead, I looked up at him and "smiled" with my eyes. He opened his eyes to watch his cock disappear into my mouth and saw me looking at him.

"I wanna fuck you, Paula," he said, sternly, his eyes drunk with desire. "I want to fuck you like you've never been fucked before, right here in this park, under this bridge."

Another twinge of pleasure surged between my thighs at just the thought of it, and I couldn't wait to feel his hard, thick cock inside of me.

I removed his dick from my mouth and stood back up, facing him. I looked down at his throbbing cock with longing. I was waiting for his instruction. I had never done anything like this before and I wasn't sure what position he was going to fuck me in. All I knew was that whatever position it was, I was going to love every minute of it.

He reached down between my legs and his fingers found my clit again. I whimpered in pleasure as he slid two fingers inside my tight, wet pussy.

"Mmm, that pussy's nice and wet for me, baby," he mumbled, his other hand stroking his still-hard cock. "I can't wait to feel that pussy on my dick."

"I want you to fuck me, Doug," I breathed, still panting from the feel of his fingers inside my twat. My whole entire body was on fire for him and I couldn't wait any longer. I wanted to feel him inside me right then.

"Turn around. I wanna see that ass," he said, his voice still raspy. "I wanna see that hot ass of yours."

I turned around and I felt him push me back up against the wall of the underpass again. I put my hands up on the wall for balance.

"Bend over, Paula," he told me, and I did as I was I told, more than willingly.

I felt his hands rubbing and massaging the cheeks of my ass. I closed my eyes, anticipating the moment when his cock would finally slide into my yearning pussy.

"Your ass is so fucking, hot, Paula, he whispered his lips mere inches away from my ear.

I felt the head of his cock rubbing up against the dripping wet entrance of my hot, pulsating cunt. I wanted him inside me—no, I needed him inside me.

"For God's sake, Doug, fuck me! Fuck me right now, please! I need to feel your cock inside me!" I cried, my eyes closed and hands against the wall.

The sun had almost completely set, and there was just a hint of light outside of the underpass. I looked back to see his cock slowly disappear as he slid the head of his cock into my pussy.

"Uhhh!" we both moaned simultaneously in pleasure as his hard, throbbing cock entered my hot, wet cunt.

"Mmm, your pussy feels so good, Paula. Ohhh, it's so tight and so wet for me!" He groaned, his lips almost touching my ear. He thrusted his cock all the way inside of me, deep down inside of my pussy until he couldn't go any deeper.

"Ah, yesss!" I cried, in passion, backing myself up and into him, forcing myself as far down on his long, hard cock as I could go. I squeezed the walls of my pussy against his dick, feeling it throb uncontrollably inside my tight cunt. I couldn't take it anymore. I wanted to cum all over his dick.

"Oh God, yes! Yes, Doug! Oh FUCK yes!" I started moving back and forth and back and forth on his hard dick, loving how it felt inside my pussy. I backed into him, over and over and over again, forcing his cock in and out of me. His dick was long and thick and hard, and it was filling every inch of me to the brim.

"Fuck, Paula! Ohh, your pussy is so fucking good!" He grabbed onto the cheeks of my ass and started pounding my pussy nice and hard from behind. With every thrust I came closer and close to my orgasm, building it up. I knew I was about to explode like never before.

"Oh yes, Doug, fuck me, baby! Oh fuck me harder. Fuck me harder, Doug, I'm gonna cum! I'm gonna cum so fucking hard, Doug!" I cried, in between huffs and puffs and moans and groans.

"Oh yes, Paula! I want you to cum on me, baby! Cum on this cock! Cum all over it, baby!" he told me, pumping into me, hard and fast, sending me further into ecstasy with every pump and every thrust.

With one final thrust, he sent me all the way over the edge and my orgasm exploded like fireworks on the Fourth of July! I came harder than I ever had before. I felt my cum juices squirt out all over his cock and I screamed out my pleasure in complete ecstasy! He was still fucking my pussy as I came, as my juices dripped down all over his hard cock. It felt soooo good! I closed my eyes and continued to cry out in delight as my orgasm peaked and then finally began to wane. It was absolute best orgasm I had ever had in my entire life. I felt drunk with pleasure.

I squeezed the walls of my pussy tight around Doug's still rock-hard cock and whimpered as the last surges of my extremely powerful and intense orgasm finally began to subside. Feeling my pussy tighten around his cock like that again, sent him completely over the edge. He couldn't take anymore.

"Ohh, Paula! I'm gonna cum! I'm gonna cum in your hot, tight wet pussy! OHHHHH!" He reached up with one hand cupped and squeezed my right breast while his other hand gripped my ass cheek, tightly. I felt him shoot his load deep inside my cunt and it felt so good! He groaned loudly as his own climax heightened. His entire body shook and stiffened, and his cock throbbed uncontrollably with every spurt of hot cum he squirted into my Pussy. He thrusted his hips against my ass cheeks with every spurt. It felt like he spurted at least 20 times.

"Oh GOD, Paula! I've never cum like that before in my life!" he whispered, panting, tiredly in my ear. He kept his cock inside me and I tightened my walls around his now-softening shaft, trying to squeeze every drop of his thick, hot cum out of his dick.

"HO...LY SHIT!" he whispered. We stayed like that for a moment, with his cock still inside me until it softened to the point where it slid out with a sloshy sound. He still stayed there hugging me from behind, with one hand on my breast and the other on my ass, resting his head on my shoulder.

I felt so good. I felt better than I'd ever felt in my entire life. It was like Doug had awakened something deep inside of me that I didn't even know was still there.

"Doug!" we heard voices calling his name.

"Oh shit, I'd better go," Doug finally said, sounding like he didn't really want to. He pulled away from me and pulled his shorts back up.

"You go ahead on, I told him. "I'm going to stay here for a moment."

With one final kiss, Doug hurried off to meet back up with his friends. I pulled my panties up and smiled. As I fixed my clothes, I could feel Doug's cum running out of my pussy and onto my panties. I knew I might not ever see Doug again, but what he'd done to me, I had a feeling things were about to change between me and my husband. He had awakened something within me and I planned to awaken the same thing in my husband when I finally made it home...

The Avengers

Jerome Petit was in a bar on Fifth Street when he saw Amanda Pierce walking into the bar. In her short mannish haircut accompanied by her confident looks, she resembled another badass cop who could crush any criminal's balls. However, that was not what crossed Jerome's mind. Jerome hated cops as he was involved in an illegal drug business. And, when he saw Amanda in her leather jacket and jeans with a badge, in sheer disgust he thought her to be a blonde slut. He keenly explored her movements while she was engaged in a small chat along with her partner with the bartender. When Amanda and her partner showed the bartender a picture and asked something, he shook his head, and so the group left. That was what surged Jerome's curiosity. Then, he   finished his drink quickly, left the bill on the table, got up and followed the group. Always having a taste for blondes, Jerome couldn't help himself to appreciate the tight pair of hemispherical ass mounds that danced rhythmically ahead of him.

As the cop group got into a sedan, Jerome watched it moving off. But Jerome never followed the car. Instead, he fell back and retarded towards the dark alley to finish his business. He was well aware of the division station's location, the shift timings of the police officers and when they change their shift. Moreover, being in the drug business for over five years, his profession taught him hard how to get prepared for work. As soon as he was done with his regular drug exchange deals in the alley, he hurried to the division station. Although he was quite far away from the division station, seated in his car, using his night vision equipment he kept a close watch on the activities of the cops, especially Amanda's. Finally, Amanda released herself of the duties and bid goodbye to her fellow colleagues. She got into a red Ford and drove home. As Jerome had never been with a cop before, he was desperate to have Amanda. Moreover, his taste for blondes also amplified his lust. Therefore, as soon as Amanda started driving home, he got into her tail.

He despised cops. But his profession had already taught him how to predict any cop movement. And, Amanda's moves were certainly the easiest ones as he knew just when she'd get off and she'd get in. Moreover, he was aware of the cases she was working on, the progress she made in the investigations and the goons she was after. Thanks to Jerome's exquisite and impeccable spy network, he also had sound knowledge about Amanda's personal life. She lived in her duplex just inside the city limits in a nice, peaceful and quiet neighborhood. She was a single mother of two kids, a boy, and a girl. A nanny always took care of the kids in her absence. But recently the nanny moved in with her as she was too busy tracking the leads on an important case. Ironically and Interestingly, Jerome was tracking Amanda's every movement for for a quite long time since she started working on the COMMODORE case.

Although Amanda's personal life was complicated, things were simpler for Jerome. This was so because Jerome knew he could get Amanda to talk if he threatened her kids. Of course, he would do no harm to the kids or to her as that was against his rules, but Amanda could never know if drug dealers had any rules as such. That night when the neighborhood was in deep sleep, Jerome broke into the house. Luckily for Jerome, Amanda's daily routine was very inflexible. As a result, Jerome knew when Amanda would have her dinner, when she would go to bed, and when she would wake up. Moreover, being an electrical genius, he had no difficulties in jamming the security systems of her home and finally sabotaged them. Thereafter, he slid into the basement through the window at midnight.

It was pitch black when Jerome broke into the basement and he knew any unexpected movements would ruin his plans. Therefore, he waited down in the basement for five-ten minutes so that his eyes would be completely adjusted to the darkness of the room. Moreover, he needed and lit a torch. Then, he padded upstairs carefully never taking his eyes away from his steps and his ears were vigilant for any subtle noise in the house. He padded further to the top floor cautiously measuring every step and slowly pushed the woman's door open. As soon as he entered the bedroom, the sweet fragrance of the room acted as a potent aphrodisiac. He couldn't steer him away from the sleeping beauty and gazed at her seductive framework. For a moment, he thought to relish every inch of her tempting lush erotica. But, he wasn't there to be involved in any sexual adventures. Instead, he was there to steal the files of the COMMODORE case.

Soon, he started to check every closet of the room for the desired object. But unfortunately, all his efforts were in vain. He was unable to track any single lead that would enable him to accomplish his desire. Frustrated at his failure and with a desperate urge to have the files regarding the case, he decided to crack Amanda the hardest way. Gradually, he crouched by the door and closed it cautiously without making a noise. The blonde temptation was deep asleep on her side with her cheek pressed into the pillow. Therefore, taking a small triangular door block from his jacket, he silently and carefully slid it beneath the door. With impeccable skills he kept it pushing hard, ensuring that any harsh sound is restricted which would awaken the sleeping beauty and ruin his plans. Certainly, he never wanted to wake up the kids, and they open the door and seeing him without his knowledge. Of course, they would do anything to rescue their mother and sabotage his plans.

He knew he had to plan his moves very carefully. Obviously, for a tough cop, it wasn't difficult to fight under these perilous circumstances. Also, he reassessed that she probably would have a decent knowledge of unarmed combat. Although Jerome was confident that his superior strengths and weight would eventually conquer Amanda, it would be imprudent and too risky on his part to make any unwanted noise that would wake up the kids downstairs. Surely, they could call the police if they found out something too fishy and dangerous. Therefore, he crawled carefully to her bed. For a moment, he was hypnotized at the tempting sight of her lush seductive framework. He watched closely how she breathed, how her body swelled and shrank as she inhaled and exhaled. Her transparent nightgown exhibited her ever sensitive and seductive curves. He couldn't help to appreciate the ravishing curves in her alluring framework. He had his hands encased in soft leather gloves and therefore he was confident not to leave his fingerprints behind. Then, he rose on the bed and gently and cautiously slid into the bed on his knees Then, moving as fast as he could and enforcing all his strengths, he clamped his left hand over her mouth. Within moments, he had turned her over onto her belly and pinned her down on the bed. Rapidly, he brought his heavy-body down on her and clutched both her wrists in his other hand. As Jerome had already cast his enormous weight on Amanda's soft body, he pinned her legs under his thighs completely baffling and immobilizing her.

The suddenness and ferocity of the circumstances and rapid succession of events bewildered Amanda beyond limits. For a moment, she froze, trying to understand if she was dreaming or was it real. As she mustered all her strengths, she sensed her perilous conditions. She struggled wildly and tried to scream. Consequently, muffled yells and screams came through Jerome's hand as her soft body squirmed beneath him. On the other hand, Jerome rode Amanda like a wild, bucking bronco waiting patiently and impatiently to settle her down or to exhaust herself. Within moments of unsuccessful struggles, Amanda realized the hopeless and helpless situation she was trapped into and yielded.

"Much better," Jerome uttered and continued softly: "Now. You and I will have to reach an understanding as per this situation, don't we?"

Amanda could only muffle in response which Jerome took for a yes.

"You don't want to wake up the kids, do you? And nothing will happen to them if you do exactly as I say", Jerome whispered intently in her ears. Then, carefully snaking his hands in his pockets and took out a handcuff, he cuffed her wrists. He took a pillow cover and ordered, "You'll take this in your mouth. Understand? Now, open your mouth". Amanda did as Jerome instructed, she could have yelled aloud awaking the kids and urging them to call for help. But she was unsure of the motives and intentions of her ardent taker and knew not how he'd react under any uncertain situation. As a result, she had no other options left but to oblige. Chilling waves splashed through her nervous system absolutely frightening and freezing her. As soon as she opened her mouth, Jerome stuffed the pillow cover as deep as he could in her mouth restricting her voices. She was on the brink of getting choked as her cheeks swelled from the stuffed cover in her mouth.

"Good girl", whispered Jerome. Thereafter, he lifted himself from her body and rolled her over, then sat back down on her hips. When Amanda stared up at Jerome, her eyes were filled with rage and fear. Her eyes couldn't believe when she gazed in sheer surprise at her ardent taker. He was the same guy about whom she was enquiring at the bar. On the other hand, Jerome was as cool as a cucumber and smiled back down at her. "Now, you probably know who I am. So, let's get straight to business. I want the COMMODORE case files?" probed Jerome intently. All Amanda could do was to respond in hate in her eyes as she was muffled. But in the most precarious and tensed up conditions of her life, she just glanced for a second at the family photo on the table just beside the bed. "Bingo!" Jerome uttered victoriously. Soon, he reached to the table and grabbed the photo frame. Studying it intently with curiosity, he opened the glass and was amazed to find a microchip in it. It was all that he was here for. As Jerome grabbed the chip and threw the photo frame aside, he smiled back at Amanda. She was breathing fast in tension and ferocity. As sweats soaked her tempting body, her seductive curves were revealed more prominently. Her eyes brimmed with rage and vengeance.

"Now, that wasn't so difficult was it, baby? So, what next? I'm going to fuck you like there's no tomorrow, and you're going to enjoy it. Understand?" yelled Jerome. An angry muffled snarl escaped Amanda's throat in response only to broaden Jerome's smile and pleasure. "Now, now. Do you want to wake up the kids?" snickered Jerome. Amanda's eyes raged in anger as she could foresee her fate. Her heart pumped like drums as her body got filled with hate and disgust. But her reactions were ineffective on Jerome. He just wanted to taste the ravishing blonde beauty whom he desired for so long. Jerome started to unbutton the enchanting beauty right in front of him. Gradually, he slid his hands onto her breasts. He mauled them, cupped them and caressed them as he couldn't help to appreciate the juicy milk buckets on her chest with the very perfect size. Jerome's touch wrecked Amanda's body like thunder. She unmindfully thought: "Am I in a dream? Should I play alone?" On the other hand, Jerome watched her face with considerable satisfaction. Amanda's pleasure organs started to erupt as his thumbs and fingers pinched her nipples hard. Her body shook with sensual excitement as he squeezed her breast. When Jerome rolled her nipples between his fingertips and pulled them hard, Amanda's sensual excitements captivated her reasoning and she yielded in her enkindled lust.

Gradually, he shifted his way down further. As he was kneeling in between her long, lanky legs, which he had forced wide apart, he had no trouble to position himself over her. She succumbed to her own buried desires when she felt Jerome's breath on her skin. He was so close that he felt the vibrations in her chest. She always wanted to try new things in the bed and this was something out of the blue experience; to be with a convict and be used like his pleasure toy. Amanda never knew that her body was so responsive and sensitive. She shivered in un-denying temptation. "Let my tongue explain how badly I crave for you" mumbled Jerome. Unable to wait any further, Jerome buried his lips on one of her chest mounds. He licked her areola lining taunting her. Then, he sucked on her nipples, softly and steadily and after that, he began biting them. As his teeth started to dig into the soft, tender meat, Amanda winced in pain. On the other hand, he constantly teased her and kept playing with her other nipple. These expert movements wreaked havoc on Amanda's lush framework and soon she was leaking from her rosebuds. While Jerome continued his foreplay, Amanda enjoyed his version of the rhythm.

Shifting further downward, he smelled the exotic aroma of her pussy. "Your legs are like an Oreo cookie. Let me split it apart and taste the cream in-between" whispered Jerome. Then, he began to lick her pussy. Prying her ever tempting cunt lips, he delved deep within her cunt lips. Electrifying sensations wreaked havoc on Amanda's body as she shivered in sensual excitement. He was not licking or sucking her rosebuds in between her legs. In fact, he was devouring the juices she excreted so passionately for him. "So, this is what it means to feel alive? Is this what it supposes to feel?" Sinful and lustful sensations conquered Amanda and all she could do was to yield to her un-denying lust. Jerome rose up like a mountain and drifted out of the bed. Calmly, and steadily yet tauntingly, he stripped before her fearful and anticipating eyes. When his giant cock sprang free from the boxers, Amanda's eyes widened and parted in awe and in anticipation of the forthcoming pleasures.

 "Yeah, baby. That's all for you", whispered Jerome as he sneered gleefully.

Thereafter, he grabbed her hair and pulled her out of bed. The night lamp was not radiant enough for Jerome to witness the ravishing radiance of his exquisite pleasure. So, he turned on the light to see her better. "Hmm, amazing curves for a cop", sneered Jerome while Amanda turned pale with fear and anguish at the unexpected turn of events. Forcing her down on her knees before him, he rubbed his hardened organ over his face. "I want you to please me like those cheap roadside sluts. Understand? So, I'm removing the muffles from your mouth. Oh! One thing, before you do something silly, do keep in mind your kids." Asserted Jerome. Gradually, Jerome removed the pillow cover stuffed deep in Amanda's mouth. As soon as Jerome did that, Amanda gasped for air and coughed violently. Jerome snickered at the pitiful sight of his fuck toy.

With no other options left, Amanda thought to oblige to the requests for her and her family's safety. Then, Jerome handed over one of the cushions off the couch and allowed Amanda to position it beneath her kneeling knees. "Now, you're comfy, eh!" Sneered Jerome. With dominant looks and silent orders, he reached out and grabbed her hair. Then, he guided her soft, luscious lips onto his hardened shaft. Since her hands were cuffed behind, all she could do to please her tormentor was to use her sultry lips. As she smelled his thick, potent and musky smell on his hardened membrane, her desires were on fire. Now, she was lusting to taste the palatable meat of a hunk holding her captive. Gradually, she opened her mouth and began to slide her tongue over his long and thick meat, lapping up his sticky and leaking juices with exquisite relish. The sensation of a pair of soft lips and tongue wrapping his cock shot electrifying sensations throughout Jerome's nervous system. As a result, he tensed and panted a little. He groaned in a low tone, and his grip on the back of Amanda's head became firmer and stiffer. Soon, Amanda like a pro tilted her head and licked up the entire length of his hardened membrane, from the base cock all the way to the head. When Amanda saw her image in Jerome's lustful eyes, she couldn't resist her eruptive horniness. While for Jerome, it was a wonderful pride moment as he had a cop on her knees serving him Without delay, Jerome grabbed Amanda in the back of her head and thrust deeper into her mouth. It was evident where he wanted her to be. Gradually,

Amanda opened her mouth and took him in, slowly and steadily, inch by inch, until he filled her completely right down to the base of her throat.

Amanda had never deepthroated anyone before. And, the intensity of her arousal coupled by her submissive state immobilized her altogether, and she tried not to gag. "You'll get used to his length", Amanda told herself as she closed her eyes tight to fight back the tears. They were watering like mad streams overflowing through the corners of her eyes moistening her soft, luscious and burning cheeks. Jerome stood still watching Amanda, his eyes filled with desire, and after a few moments, she had recovered enough to continue. Bobbing her head up and down over Jerome's thick and potent shaft at a leisurely pace, Amanda allowed her tongue to move languidly against the smooth underside of his cock. "My God," Jerome groaned, still playing with her hair now as her head moved up and down on his shaft. "Fuck, you're a slut. You surely, know how to give a deepthroat. You're dying to have me explode in your mouth, aren't you?" He concluded. He was smooth, quick and slick against her tongue. And now she could taste his leaking juices right in the back of her throat. Thicker and denser than before, the salty taste of the leaking potent juices filled her mouth revealing his growing arousal. It was delightfully delicious, and she allowed her tongue to move greedily over the underside of his shaft. Soft sultry moans escaped her throat now as her pussy began to clench with undeniable cravings.

Jeremy looked like a man completely overpowered by his own desire. Soon, Amanda's cheeks and throat started to ache as the length of the shaft was too much for Amanda's mouth to continue for long. So, she stopped her back-and-forth motion for a moment, taking the time to envelop the head of his membrane lovingly. She drooled on her juicy tits like one of those porn stars acting in porn. However, Amanda was surprised and spellbound at the retention ability of Jerome; anyone else would have exploded in her mouth overwhelmed by her impeccable skills. Taking him in her mouth once again, Amanda resumed her deep-throating services again so that his hardened pole touched the bottom of her throat. "If my hands weren't tied, I would have proved my exquisite skills more efficiently", Amanda thought unmindfully.

Suddenly, his hands, which had been moving leisurely through her hair, stopped their movements, and she sensed the muscles of his legs tightening around her. Within seconds he had toughened completely, and pumped his hips back and forth, driving his kingly shaft deeper into her throat. He had grabbed her head so tightly that she felt her mouth was being used as a cunt. All Amanda could do was to moan in strangled gurgling sounds. Loads and loads of saliva dribbled over his shaft lubricating it while she felt his overwhelming stokes in the back of her throat. Soon, he made a loud moan and then hot streams of protein shake began pumping down the back of her throat. The intensity of his ecstatic orgasm was indicated by his squeezed eyes and absolutely shut, and his head thrown back in ecstasy. Watching him, Amanda swallowed every drop of his protein juices relishing the taste of his blissful orgasm. Once he was done, he lay very still on the couch with his head leaned back desperately trying to catch his breath. As for Amanda, she coughed and gagged spilling the residue fluids that she couldn't swallow. She was too tired to make her move. She was too exhausted and frightened to take advantage of the situation and escape from the clutches of the convict. Yet, mustering all her strengths, she jumped to her feet and ran towards the bedroom door. In sheer desperation, she pressed her back against it and tried to turn the knob using her cuffed hands. But all her desperate efforts were in vain. She tried to scream but couldn't. On the other hand, Jerome regained his strengths and senses. His shaft was still as hard as ever, probably, hornier at the hopeless efforts of a captive cop. He padded over slowly as she desperately attempted to open the door. He took the long, thick nightstick in his hand and thrashed on her large hemispherical scoop like ass mounds. It planted a large red streak on her alabaster white ass cheeks as she writhed in agonizing pain on the floor. As soon as Amanda tried to scream, Jerome muffled her mouth tightly using the pillow cover and hissed: "Careful slut! You don't want to commit a silly mistake, do you?"

Then, he gripped her mannish hair and pulled her away from the door. Forcing her across the room, he pushed her against her dresser furniture and pulled out a chair from the vicinity. When he settled down on the chair, she was leaning against her dresser and stared at her tormentor in sheer terror.

"What next, cop girl? We've just got started. So come over here and drop your cunt down on my pole here. You're going to do all the pleasure work for me, and make sure you do well as you did with your mouth. Understand?" asserted Jerome. Amanda nodded in acknowledgment.

Holding his kingly shaft up for her, he smiled intently and gestured her. "Come on, slut," he snapped. As Amanda shuffled forward, her body shook in fear and in terrified anticipation of the next chain of events. Again, as she widened her legs and straddled the chair, she squirmed, and her eyes once again got filled hatred for the convict. Jerome held his kingly shaft upright as Amanda squatted above it and lowered her gently. Jerome was growing increasingly impatient at the slow unfolding of events. So, he grabbed her hips and forced her against his. Recognizing his tormentor's severe urge to pin her down, Amanda jerked up briefly and sensed his cock tip against her slit. As soon as the kingly member touched the lips of her tight vagina, the electrifying sensation shivered her body making her knees weak. As a result, she started to get fully and rapidly impaled by the shaft. Gradually, she sank down and his thick fuck pole slid up into her belly.

When her juicy and overflowing pussy had just consumed three-fourths of the shaft, she shuddered and groaned. Probably, it was too much for her at one go, so she tried to rise again. Sensing her moves, Jerome sniggered and grabbed her ass mounds. Thereafter, he started to jerk her down as he thrust up. Inch after inch of polished, well salivated and lubricated fuck pole jammed her cunt tunnel until the whimpering lady cop was forced to the toes by the thrust from underneath against her guts. Amanda creamed on the potent pole like hell and she felt captivating sensations flooding her body.

"Bet you haven't experienced this on your pussy for a long time. Have you, slut?" he hissed. Muffled screams escaped her throat as Jerome's shaft conquered her pit. He shoved his meat deep into her guts and her ass cheeks flattened against his thighs. Jerome gave her little time to recover and adjust to his gigantic pole. As she began to lower and raise herself on the thick membrane, erotic and sensual moans made their way through her throat. Soon, Amanda's up and down, humping gained a rhythmic pace and she was sliding her pussy up and down on his thick organ. "Oh! My God! What's that monster doing to me? I can feel my walls stretched beyond limits", Amanda thought unmindfully as she ground her hips onto him. Jerome never missed a chance to taunt her seduction and pressed her soft melons against his face. Sucking, licking, biting, he did perform his actions with impeccable skills that sent Amanda to pleasure heights of the highest heaven.

"That's right, babe! That's how I stretch my girl and they cream over my shaft. I'm going to ruin that tight little pussy good. Understood slut?" hissed Jerome as he pumped from beneath. Amanda never enjoyed a quiet, sensible sort of love. She always craved to be devoured, and this experience felt likewise. Despite her degradation, Amanda was now experiencing sensational excitements that she couldn't control.

"You're one fine piece of ass," Jerome concluded. In his commanding tone, he evidently groped and fondled the blonde woman's lush ass cheeks. Amanda did not know how to respond. Her pussy was on the verge of experiencing a blissful excitement. She sensed the tension building up in her cavity. Gradually, she also sensed a subsequent tension on Jerome's pole. Within moments, he pumped loads of steamy milk into her pussy. The excitement was too extreme for Amanda to withstand and she succumbed to her desires and crossed her limits. Although a part of her mind confronted her about the sin, a more perverted part provoked her excitement. Finally, their bodies entwined in exhaustion and greater were the fatigue in Jerome. The euphoria of blissful orgasm almost rendered Jerome senseless and this was the moment for Amanda.

Now, slowly and steadily she lifted herself from his shaft. Although excessively tired, Amanda mustered her remaining strengths and padded in front of Jerome. Cautiously, she reached for her hairpins in her dressers. Once she had one, she used it with impeccable skills to set herself free from the handcuffs. "Bingo," she told herself. By the time Jerome gained his strengths and opened his eyes, Amanda was well prepared with her handgun and was sitting right in front of him. Ferocious vengeance engulfed her mind and she pointed the gun at Jerome with extreme prejudice. "I'm not the cop to scare convicts with threats. I plot my revenge silently." Thus, she fired six shots and emptied the magazine. Finally , the gun fell from her hands; she trembled at her own overwhelming success. She dialed 911 and stated: "Amanda Pierce here. I've shot COMMODORE Jerome." And she disconnected the call. 15-20 minutes later, she heard sirens outside her house.

One Turn

Some people might think that NI (Natural Insemination) is a lusty way for a man to get sex. It can be, but if done correctly it is actually a reliable delivery method for the sperm into the woman. Some prefer the deliver to be at a doctor's office with the doctor placing the sperm at the cervix and getting you pregnant. Others try it themselves with various methods (turkey basters, etc.). NI is starting to gain popularity among women who want a more relaxed, natural way to conceive rather than at a doctor's office.

I'm a firm believer in NI and my husband and I have been involved in natural donations to lesbian couple. Yes, it did involve sex but it was not a sex orgy, but a wonderful experience to watch. This couple was desperate for children and had tried the medical route several times, but it just didn't work. They then decided to go at it themselves to save on the cost and had tried inseminating using the old fashioned turkey baster using donated sperm from a male, gay friend. This again didn't work and they began to wonder what else they could do.

They began doing research and began to come to the realization that good old fashioned sexual intercourse with a man would probably be the way to go. It offered the highest chance to become pregnant, especially if done during the fertile week. The research indicated that some woman chose their most fertile day and had sex. Others had sex twice. The method with the best results, according to their research, of having intercourse four times during the fertile week.

They finally decided to choose to have intercourse four times during her fertile week. Through lesbian websites on how to get pregnant, they found that the best way (if you just had to use NI) was for the couple to make love beforehand to get the "juices" flowing before introducing the man who would enter the woman and ejaculate, but do little else. It sounded easy enough for them and they decided to do it. But the problem now where to find a willing man.

That's where we came in. We had met them socially a few years back and found that they like to do some of the same activities that we did. But we eventually lost contact when they moved to a different part of town. We met again by accident at an event and we went out to eat with them afterwards. We talked about everything and they soon let it slip that what they were planning. I was taken back a bit since I had never heard of this.

Sure, I knew some women purposely on "accident" got pregnant now and then when they wanted a baby and were single, but to be so bold as to do what they were planning floored me.

Now, before I go on, I want to say that my husband and I are no prudes. I'm in my middle 50's and my husband is 15 years younger than me. We have been married 8-years and have never been happier. We have also experimented ourselves, now and then, with other partners (with the full consent of each other). I wouldn't call ourselves swingers or that we have a truly open marriage, but we aren't opposed to experimenting.

So that being said, I was still floored that they would even consider this. I asked them about how they would find a man, how would they know his medical background, what if he turned out to be a weirdo who wanted access to the child later on? I didn't mean to spray water on their plan, and when I saw their faces start to droop, I apologized and tried to be positive about it. My only warning to them was to be careful and chose carefully.

We continued talking about other things and then just before we left, one of the women said jokingly (though I know today it wasn't a joke) what if my husband could be the donor. We laughed about and went home. On the way home I asked my husband (in a half way joke) what he thought about being a donor. He laughed and said that he would love to do it to help them out. That was the beginning of baby Jonathan.

We kept in contact with the lesbian couple and went out a few more times with them. On the third outing during a quiet spell, I asked them how things were going with their search. They looked down hearted and said that it seems impossible to find anyone. I then saw one of the women shed a single tear and I told her I was sorry for bring this up. They said it has been hard for them since making the decision to go this way. They both were upset that all the other preferred methods didn't work and that this last, best opportunity wasn't going anywhere.

My heart was breaking for them which is what made me blurt out that perhaps my husband would be willing to be the donor. That took them back and I could see their minds calculating the offer. They asked me several times if I was serious, and hating to speak for my husband, I went out on the limb and told them that I was. They began to chat excitedly with each other and then to me. They asked me a million questions about my husband's background and health. I assured them that he was very healthy and didn't have any family history of medical problems (well his mother did have very bad bunions on her feet). I told them that my husband could also undergo a complete medical to their satisfaction.

I then looked over at my husband who was by the pond of the Japanese garden examining the architecture and its general appearance and felt a twinge of guilt that I was in the middle of negotiating his genetic future. Well, I assured myself, he won't mind. I finally got around asking the couple which of them was the one wanting to get pregnant and one of them blushed and said it was her. They actually both were fairly good looking and either could have been the one ready to carry a child.

I told them that we all needed to go home and think this out and we agreed to meet the next day for coffee to discuss the matter again, if we still wanted to go through with it. I called for my husband, who came trotting over, and I held his hand and we all continued walking through the garden.

We all first sat down and discussed ground rules. There would be no kissing, no oral sex, no fondling. That would be done by the couple themself. This couple was not swingers, so were not used to the idea of being watched during sex.

The way it worked was that we went to the couple's home and were cooked a wonderful meal. We then talked about what was going to happen and made sure everyone was still comfortable. My husband was then asked to shower and put on a rob the couple had bought for him. He did as he was told and as he was doing so, the other couple went to their bedroom and began making love. When my husband got out of the shower he went into the living room with me and we sat there nervously waiting for the other couple.

Soon, a voice shouted to us that they wanted me to get my husband "ready." This wasn't hard as he was already fairly hard and it only took a few touches to get him to attention. They had also asked that I first wash my hands and do no oral on him, to keep the germs away. I complied and gently stroked my husband.

About ten minutes later we hard a voice calling us into the bedroom. I was also invited in and took my seat at the couch. The woman who was going to receive my husband's donation was in a loose rob that covered her and her head was in the lap of her partner who was dressed also in a robe.

My husband was handed a tube of lubricant and while he got ready, the partner put some lube on her finger and I saw her hand disappear between her partner's legs which were still hidden underneath the robe, to lube up her vagina entrance.

The partner with the head in her lap then began to talk gently to the partner about to receive my husband's sperm and told her not to be nervous and to think of their baby. I could tell that they were still very nervous, so I had my husband sit down next to me on the loveseat and waited while the woman was calmed down.

I was wondering if we should just leave since it didn't seem like it was going to happen. I then began to make conversation and joked a bit to try and lighten up the mood. That seemed to work as they both smiled and I could see them both relaxing a bit. I suggested that we don't do anything yet, but just talk which they readily agreed to. The partner not receiving the donation said she would love to talk over a glass of wine and she got up and went into the kitchen and came back with an open bottle of red wine and poured us each a glass. It did the trick as it opened everyone up.

My husband even was able to joke a when he asked with a smile if they were sure they wanted a baby with all of the midnight feedings and having to stay home at night. This made them laugh and I could see that they were thinking about this and they both turned to each other and said that this is really something they have both wanted for so long.

We finished our wine and the couple turned to each other and nodded. The one about to receive the donation said, "I'm being ridiculous. We both want a baby and this is our opportunity." With that she asked partner to sit near her head so she could place her head in her lap. Once done she pulled her partner's hands underneath her robe where I could tell she was getting her ready.

I did the same to my husband, but I purposely let his robe open up more than it should so he penis could be observed. They were both slightly embarrassed, but I believe this had the benefit and getting them over their nervousness. About ten minutes of touching our respective spouses and the woman receiving the donation flung open her robe and exposed her body. She then bent up her knees and parted her legs and said that she was ready. She also half-way joked that it's been awhile since she had a man inside of her, so be gently.

My husband got up, opened up his rob exposing his front, but kept it on. He was handed the lubricant again which he used to spread liberally over his male member and handed it back to the partner with holding the head in her lap. She then placed some lubricant on her partners entrance and said, "Let's do this. " My husband went over to the woman lying before him and got between her legs. He was smart enough not to move around too much but waited for her to get used to him being there. I then saw the woman with the head in her lap nod her head which was the signal for my husband, who took hold of his penis and place it at the entrance of the woman. He moved it around a bit and then pushed in. He was slow, but sure and it took about 30 seconds for his entire p e nis to disappear inside the woman's vagina.

My husband then positioned himself so that he was standing between her legs and he took hold of her hips and began to gently thrust. I'm surprised my husband didn't orgasm right there, but the waiting and the glass of wine helped him to last. I'm not sure if the lesbian couple wanted that, but it didn't really matter.

So, here I am in another couples bedroom watching my husband impregnating another woman. I have to admit I was turned on, but I couldn't do anything but watch. I was watching sex, but it was void of any real compassion. As agreed, there was no touching except in the few agreed upon areas (like the hips) and of course no kissing. I could hear the woman panting, but I think it was more in anticipation of getting pregnant than of actual pleasure.

It seemed like they were going at it for a very long time, but actually it was only about five minutes. I then heard my husband say that he was about to come and his thrusting became quicker until I heard him panting and then saw his body as he began twitching as he made his release into the woman. He stayed inside her for a few more moments before he pulled out. The woman that had just received his sperm immediately turned around and placed her barefeet high into the air and resting on the bedframe. The other partner explained that they wanted the sperm to stay inside her as long as possible.

We all sat and talked, with our robes closed back up and watched the woman with her feet in the air. We then talked about the next donation, which was going to be the next evening. As I said before, they had made some studies and had elected to have sex four times during her most fertile time, instead of just once or twice. This was bad news for me since I wouldn't be able to have sex for the next four days.

We finally said our goodbyes and left. We got home and my husband showered. When he got out he pulled me toward him and kissed me. Though we couldn't have sex, we did have some wonderful cuddling and he gave me some wonderful oral sex.

The next day the couple called us. I was half expecting them to opt out of the next baby making session, but they were even more excited than before. They were calling to make sure that we would be over that evening. After I told them that they would be, the head partner told me to expect things to go much easier now that the initial sex had taken place and they could relax.

That evening we arrived and found the in a happy mood, totally different from the previous night. They again asked my husband to take a shower while they prepared themselves. My husband did as he was told and came out a little while later wearing the same robe (but washed) and came to the living room to join me. We could hear the other couple in the bedroom, but this time the door wasn't shut and we could hear some moaning and groaning going on.

My husband was soon summoned and as we both entered the bedroom, we saw that they were both smiling, relaxed, and ready to go. This time a bottle of wine was ready for us and we again had our single glass and talked for a few minutes before the donation time.

My husband was handed the lubricant and he quickly put it on and the other woman did the same. They positioned themselves like they did before, with the woman's head in her lap and she opened up her robe without hesitation, bent her knees and spread wide her legs. My husband repeated his performance for last night and entered her.

He again lasted about five minutes which is when I heard his telltale noises that told me he was close to an orgasm. Sure enough he came and I saw the woman who was receiving the deposit with her eyes closed smiling. She was breathing very deeply and seemed very content.

She once again placed her feet on the bedpost and after we talked for awhile we left, being reminded of course of our appointment tomorrow. We went home where I was again given a good cuddling and oral.

The couple called again like clockwork to make sure we would be there again, and of course I told them that we would. We arrived on time and again, my husband made his deposit as always. The next day was going to be our last. I was glad to get this over as I missed having my own husband to myself.

We arrived for our final and last time and this time the mood seemed very cheerful. They cooked us a nice meal and we sat and chatted a bit before they asked my husband to take his shower. They excused themselves and went into the bedroom. My husband soon came out to join me and we sat there listening to the noises of lovemaking. I heard an unusually load moan and realized that one of them was having an orgasm. On the previous times they were making love but it seemed they were doing it only to get the woman who was going to receive my husband wet. This time it seemed like a full blow session.

We were invited in and immediately saw that both women were nude. The main partner told us, "We feel like you are part of the family. We very much want to thank you for what you've done for us." With that she got up and put on her robe, but the other woman made no effort to dress but just laid there. The other woman came up to my wife and asked if it would be all right for them both to have full body contact sex since this will be the last time. She assured me that there would be no kissing, oral, breast sucking. It would still be straight intercourse, but in the missionary position. She explained that she wanted to make this last time really count and that this was the best position to get pregnant in.

I agreed and the woman and I both sat down on the couch to watch. The woman bent up her knees and spread her legs as before and I saw her put lubricant between her legs. She handed my husband the lubricant and he did the same. He then turned and looked at both of us and mouthed, "OK?" We both nodded our heads and he turned to the woman on the bed, bot between her legs, but instead of standing on the floor while he entered her, this time he got up onto the bed properly, got on top of the woman properly. I then watched as his penis tried to find its mark and the woman reached down and guided him inside of her.

Though they were not kissing, the sight of my husband naked and on top of another woman was an amazing thing to watch. Because this was the fourth time my husband had sex in as many days, he was able to last a long time inside of her. They didn't change positions but kept going in the missionary position. He last about 15-minutes before I could tell he was getting close. She then asked him to push off her a bit and she then reached down and began to stimulate her clitoris.

This was new since I thought that they both didn't want too much pleasure. The other woman saw my looks and told me that they both wanted a boy, and that having an orgasm makes the body more acidy, which benefits the "boy" sperm. I asked her why they didn't do this before, and they said that it was because her partner was too nervous to have an orgasm, even when they both had sex together before my husband came into the room. She explained that this was the first time she was able to orgasm, so they thought that maybe she could orgasm during sex with my husband. Since they were limited to intercourse only, stimulating the clitoris with her finger was the best option.

It seemed to work because the woman was fingering her clitoris with vigor and had her eyes tightly closed. When she came, my husband lost it and made his last and final release inside of her. He kept pumping inside her for awhile and then got out. The woman quickly placed her feet onto the bedpost again and seemed very relaxed and happy. I don't know if it was the fact that she was happy with the orgasm or happy to get it over with.

Now we had to see if it would work. But that would take a month or so. We finally said our goodbyes and left. Well we got word from the couple that it had worked and that a pregnancy had occurred and they were over joyed. My husband was a bit disappointed that it had worked so fast since he was half expecting to be summoned again very soon. Well it was not to be.

Nine months later baby Jonathan was born.

Beautiful Chains

Nalia wants to sleep at bliss. She awakened in darkness and chains. The young witch shook her head, attempting to clear the fog out of her head. The last thing she recalled. She'd used the banned ritual to summon the demon Raum. And he'd seduced her, attempting to get his liberty. That was not quite perfect. She'd seduced him too, hoping to produce the demon violate his contract. And.

Then they'd finished up in each other arms making love till the morning. She recalls Raum running his hands through her sweat-soaked reddish hair as she'd clutched desperately into his lithe, muscled chest.

Nalia's eyes were starting to adapt to the darkness. And somehow, she had been here. Can she do it? Had Raum chased her? As she watched the area trying to find a recognizable hint, she ran a hand on her clothing.

Her black witch's robe was gone replaced with a very simple cotton skirt which fell on her knees and also a very simple smock. Nalia understood enough to comprehend a mobile when she watched it.

A mattress, a chamber pot, chains, along with an iron door. Someone did not want her departing. She did not need to wait to learn who. Soft footsteps echoed down the hallway, stopping in her doorway. The door swung open easily, and a woman entered. She had been a couple of years younger than Nalia with brown hair which bobbed if she transferred. The woman bowed awkwardly her bangs falling around her eyes as she clutched her white cotton robe.

"I'm sister Eliza. Please come together."

Nalia believed a rage building inside her. The sisters of mild may believe that they could smack several chains onto a loaf and call it a day, however, Nalia had electricity they hadn't ever wanted. Reaching out with her thoughts, Nalia caught the woman's character and chucked her body throughout the room just like a ragdoll.

Or, that is exactly what she attempted to do. What really happened was Nalia achieved with her head and that she fell screaming into the floor. She could not breathe; she could not think. The fire burnt into her throat, searing her throat closed. Sister Eliza hurried on her side.

"Please, don't hurt yourself" The woman's voice had actual concern within it.

It required all of Nalia's power simply to nod. The pain was gone now, but her body was quivering.

"It is the collar" Eliza explained, busying herself unleashing Nalia's manacles.

"The sisters also have sealed your abilities. Attempt to utilize them, and you'll be punished."

"Great to know," Nalia handled as Eliza assisted the sorceress into her toes.

When she recovered her power, maybe she can overpower Eliza, however, for now, she had been helpless as a kitten.

Eliza assisted Nalia down a lean, rock hallway. By a couple of the rooms that they passed, Nalia can here yell and yells. "Don't worry."

Eliza ensured her seeing the look in her head.

"They're being purified, repenting in the wicked ways."

Nalia felt her throat go dry. "Is that what is likely to happen to me? I'm likely to be purified?" Eliza nodded solemnly.

"It's the destiny of the evil."

"And Raum, what about Raum?" Nalia did not really understand why she inquired. Exactly what exactly did she really care what happened to a demon she chose randomly out of a book?

However, she found herself dangling on Eliza's words.

"Raum?" Eliza wrinkled her brow. "Oh, so you mean that the demon spawn." She shook her head. Nalia felt her heart leap into her throat. "nobody has purified a demons' pawn before." Viewing Nalia's face, Eliza attempted to reassure her.

"However, Sister Lily, our experienced purifier, is about the endeavour. If anybody can do it, then she could."

"How many... how many has Sister Lily purified?"

"Dozens. She is an inspiration for all." Eliza lowered her voice conspiratorially.

"They say she's never neglected. Not once. Can you feel that?"

"And you?" Nalia asked, trusting. "Me" Eliza paused.

"I... This is my very first purification. Please forgive my lapses." Nalia was not certain what to say to this, but Eliza spared a reply by opening among those many iron doors which lined the hallway. The objective of the area was unmistakable.

Even the Red Witches had lots of such chambers. Interrogation chambers they euphemistically named them. Torture implements lined the walls. Long whips, brief whips, barbed whips, iron maidens of sizes and shapes, and much more. The majority of the apparatus; however, Nalia couldn't name. Each of them looked cruel, however.

"This way, please."

Eliza explained as she picked her way through the maze of tables, chains, and seats, all adorned with a range of manacles and spikes. "Here. Please"

She gestured into a wooden horse; then a believe wooden triangle place five feet off the floor. Nalia eyed the apparatus apprehensively. She had been feeling better today, possibly powerful enough to conquer Eliza. The younger woman felt her hesitation.

"Please, I really do not need to hurt you."

Eliza raised her hands, and Nalia believed her collar start to heat.

"You need to know; you can't oppose me. The collar has been commanded by my own will. Should I want it, then you may perish" Nalia believed.

Not only was that the woman apparently incapable of deception, however, but it also was not the only way that they could control their offenders. Obediently, the sorceress mounted on the wooden horse.

She can feel the sharp border pushing from her heart. Uncomfortably, she pushed her hands to ease some of their strain. Eliza moved definitely, no more the nervous woman she had been at the hallway. She procured all Nalia's legs, bending them back till her knees touched her elbows and hauling them tightly with rope.

Nalia did not bother resisting, anything Eliza had intended for her could occur with or without the permission. Twin ropes secured Nalia's ankles for her thighs and jumped her knees, forcing her thighs at a kneeling posture. Without a place to locate buy, her thighs were not anything more than sandbags, pushing her whole body weight on where her fulcrum fulfilled the wooden horse.

"Does that hurt?" Eliza requested, procuring the previous rope.

"Just a bit."

"That is to be expected. Hands please"

Nalia shook her head.

"My palms..." she tried lamely to describe.

Her palms were the one thing maintaining the complete weight of her own body out of pressing between her thighs.

"Shh, I understand."

Eliza reassured her earlier a bolt of flame burst Nalia's neck. The result was instant; Nalia's body pitched on her muscles.

Her wrists were limp while her wrists clutched the horse as though it had been her fan. She found himself gasping for air, not able to withstand as Eliza lifted her palms and procured them at manacles that dangled over her head.

"You know; this is essential if we want to treat you."

Eliza appeared to be more reassuring herself over Nalia.

"Heal me... of what?"

Nalia gasped. Since the darkness of pain started to recede, Nalia might feel the entire force of this wooden horse shoving her legs, through her underclothes, and seeking to divide her lips.

"Why, your wickedness naturally."

"However, what have I done?" Eliza shrugged.

"Included in this purification procedure you may acknowledge your evil deeds."

Sensation has been coming into Nalia now.

She could sense her arms stretched over her head, the rope which pieces into her thighs, the cold perspiration trickling down her underarms, anything to keep her head off the monster between her thighs. She attempted to shift stance, but the monster was constant, nuzzling and shoving farther if she shifted her every movement, making her position worse.

"Connect me," Eliza asked, "because we all pray for the four evils that have to be purified." "Four?" Nalia responded, not entirely certain she wanted to understand.

Eliza nodded solemnly.

"Four evils reside inside every fallen girl. Your heart" Eliza touched Nalia's breastfeeding. "Your womanhood." Eliza touched reduced on Nalia's midsection. "Your sanity" She touched on Nalia's lips.

"And..." Eliza trailed off. "And what?" "And..." Eliza touched Nalia's buttocks,

"Your bliss

"Nalia did not enjoy the noise of some of the.

"Can I get a charm?" Eliza shook her head. "The hens have announced that you are guilty. There's not any greater authority. Whenever you're purified, you'll thank me" Nalia sighed. Obviously. "But we have to quantify your wickedness."

 For whatever reason, Eliza appeared to be blushing.

The priestess achieved forward grasping the throat of Nalia's cotton smock. With a jolt, she snapped it open. Nalia squirmed because her breasts spilt out. Squirming she strove to resist, however, her palms hung over her head and her wrists tied, she had been helpless as Eliza peeled off her top. Naked from the waist upward Nalia can just observe as Eliza murmured appreciatively, running a hot finger on Nalia's tight shoulder blades and then down her flanks.

She stopped to the tight muscles from Nalia's tummy, pressing them lightly.

"I feel there is much worse in you" A hand pushed down Nalia's shoulder and she gasped as the wooden horse pushed its way further between her thighs.

"Can you believe that?" Eliza requested.

"This is the annoyance of your wickedness." Eliza ran a hand within Nalia's exposed breasts. Cupping every person in turn. "Can you find that?" Eliza whispered to her ear.

"There's the evidence you have to be purified." Nalia chased her traitorous nipples.

Her entire body had betrayed her, reacting automatically to Eliza's delicate touch. They strained to your priestess's signature. And Eliza was too pleased to oblige.

Her hands circled Nalia's nipples, teasing her delicate breasts and delivering waves of pleasure. A tough twist created that the sorceress scream and writhe, the atmosphere is torn out of her throat. Nalia braced herself to get longer, but Eliza looked fulfilled, moving to her next goal.

Her right hand caught Nalia's short hair, and her left hand leaned the sorceress's face upward. Instantly, until Nalia could grasp exactly what was occurring, Eliza brought her lips shut. This moment Nalia gasped in surprise instead of pain since Eliza's tongue found hers. Her lips tasted like peanuts. Her tongue tasted candy.

Nalia blinked in confusion. She was not, she had not, definitely not with Eliza. However, the heat spreading through her torso gave the lie to this confusion. Her entire body had no qualms recognizing exactly what her brain-boggling whatsoever.

Nalia, not able to control himself felt her mouth meeting Eliza's cheeks, tasting her tongue working her mouth from Eliza's. After what seemed like an eternity, Eliza pulled back softly. Nalia's mouth attempted to follow along with unwillingly to go. The younger woman took a minute to collect herself as she ran her tongue across her lips.

"There's a lot of wickedness there too. And you're delicious." For after, Nalia could just nod in agreement. What has been happening? Unexpectedly she approached Eliza in a fresh light. The brief, brown-haired priestess wore a cotton robe which did little to hide her curves. Nalia can see the woman's nipples poking,

Could run down her eyes Eliza's buttocks thighs. Could see that the flush round Eliza's the equally stylish neck. Apparently, Nalia was not the sole evil one. "One final evaluation, and after that, the purification begins," Eliza transferred into the walls of whips. Nalia saw her every movement.

The woman went like moonlight, and the sorceress could not tear her eyes away

Eliza's softly rocking waist. She licked her lips, imagining the joy she can bring this woman. What exactly was wrong with her? Eliza chosen a brief leather-wrapped with a couple or so knotted lashes.

A cat o' nine tails if Nalia recalled the title correctly. Eliza was no stranger into the gadget. She hefted it readily, running along its length and then twisting the lashes around her palms.

"When you're purified, you'll forgive me."

Nalia tensed as Eliza vanished, trying to prepare herself for the blow which she knew was coming. But even so, she let out a shout once the whip landed a stinging blow on her flank.

Eliza struck hard enough that she didn't break the skin, leaving rows of reddish lash marks. Another shout once the whip struck between her shoulders. Her lower spine. Nalia's breath was ragged, but Eliza was only starting. Her whip discovered that the sorceress's tummy, then her tender breasts.

Nalia sensed her eyes blur tears because the sharp reddish welts functioned through her entire body. Nalia sobbed helplessly because the potency jumped from her physique. With each blow, she needed down on the wooden horse. With each blow, she may sense the delight seeping through her entire body.

She did not understand when it occurred, possibly when Eliza kissed her, then possibly once the lash landed in her rear, possibly the horse was banging her creature desires. Everything Nalia did realize was that her lips were dripping wet, parting voluntarily, nearly begging, such as the timber to press farther. She understood that each lash, every shout, had been bringing her closer to bliss.

Nalia's body has been flush with joy, and each single time Eliza struck by her whip, and her hips involuntarily bucked. After the lashes discovered her nipples, then she can hardly control himself. The mixture of pleasure and pain was addictive, such as no feeling she'd ever believed. She elevated her breasts to satisfy up with the blow then shrieked if it obtained sending a tide a flame and then a tide of delight.

And each time she bucked. She tried to dismiss it, to deny it, however, the electrical jolts of pleasure out of her pussy couldn't be refused. She had been happy to get something between her thighs, so happy to get anything pushing her cunt, and that she needed more. Needed more. Eliza diverse her rate, created Nalia wait, so unsure of if the next blow will fall.

A hand followed the dimple beneath her arm, then squeezed her hands ever so gently, then a series of leather captured her breast.

"You shout beautifully."

Eliza understood. Somehow, despite it all, she understood. This Nalia was hooked on this pain, fed it off, desired more. "More, please. Only slightly more."

Nalia was nearly there, and her buttocks were rocking together with the rhythm which could bring her candy release, just a couple more strikes. However, Eliza had other thoughts. She attained between Nalia's legs. Helpless to prevent her, then the sorceress observed in terror as Eliza lifted her skirt away from her underclothes, and put her cold hands on Nalia's burning hot clit.

She could sense it today, visit Nalia's burning appetite, any doubts she may have had were disappeared. Only her signature compelled Nalia's body push forward, hoping to find more.

"Not only, my keen friend." Eliza smiled, "However, I will understand there is a lot of bad in you. The purification can start." Nalia shuddered.

If the purification had been anything such as this, she'd lose her head, a servant to her lusts. She couldn't let this happen. Summoning all her strength, Nalia left her very last gambit.

"And what about you? It appears there's much wickedness in you too, Sister Eliza." On Nalia's surprise, the woman nodded sadly.

"I fear I like this ritual too much. When it's over, I have to turn myself for punishment."

"Imagine if... what if..." Nalia hunted desperately.

This is it she understood, and this could be her only way out.

"Imagine if, I purified you so you wouldn't need to face punishment."

Eliza's face lit up but darkened with feeling.

"You understand that the purification rituals? You wouldn't irritate me?" Nalia managed a feeble grin,

"I can't betray you, that the collar remains around my throat. Along with the Red, Witches possess lots of purification rituals. Some stronger than your own." She had her today.

"Stronger? What will the Red Witches understand of eliminating evil?"

"Allow me to show you" Eliza hesitated, then nodded.

"The ritual is likely to be more powerful if I'm pure of body and mind. What should I perform?"

The priestess undid Nalia's bindings, softly massaging her legs, arms, and legs as she did this. Even totally free, Nalia may feel her own body's heat, a nice feeling that ebbed if she ceased to examine Eliza's ideal shoulders. Her body cried out for the launch. Not today, she thought, only a little while more.

"What should I perform?" Eliza requested the nervous woman that Nalia had met producing her return. Nalia was uncomfortably conscious of her exposed torso. Giving orders into somebody wearing more clothing than she felt odd and out of place.

Taking a deep breath, then she smoothed her skirt, her final shred of modesty also tried her commanding voice.

"If you're supposed to be purified, then you need to use the uniform of the penitent."

Nalia explained slowly, imagining at the appropriate words.

"Eliminate that emblem of the pure."

Eyes filled with doubt, Eliza undid the strings binding her robe closed and allow it to slip to the floor. Beneath the priestess wore nothing in any way. Nalia allows her gaze linger to the younger woman's body. Yes, she desired that she'd have this. The sorceresses' requirement was nearly palpable. How can it not be Nalia believed?

Eliza's little, enthusiastic breasts have been flushed with desire. Her shorts fulfilled in an ideal 'U' representing her pale brown curls. Her feet curled beautifully, promising untold delights. On a hunch, Nalia places her hands between Eliza's legs.

The woman squeaked in dread and humiliation as Nalia's hands found her slickness. Eliza's legs have been coated inside her desire.

"There's a lot of wickedness in you."

Nalia intoned as her hands carefully researched Eliza's celestial opening.

"Lick." Nalia controlled, bringing her hands around Eliza's face. The priestess's eyes opened wider.

"No... no..." Nalia left her head sadly.

"It's is the only means. You analyzed my wickedness, did you not? Today you need to test your personal."

That was sufficient. Eliza's mouth leaned forward, final on all Nalia's hands in turn.

"And?" "There's..." Eliza stuttered,

"There's much wickedness in me."

"Mmmm, there's indeed. Did you like that? Don't lie."

Eliza nodded.

"We have to stem the wave."

Nalia knelt down, motioning to get Eliza to appear nearer. Eliza squeaked in surprise since Nalia's tongue found her plump, moist lips.

"I have... I have never... with a woman.

" Nalia might have confessed that neither had she had, however, she had any thoughts and she was not convinced she could quit her tongue if she wished to. Her hands gently massaged Eliza's waist, pressing ever so slightly on her stomach. Her tongue danced about Eliza's clit; she had been rewarded with a gasp whenever it touched.

Eliza's own body quivered in Nalia's signature; the woman showed her feelings just like a publication. Also, Nalia shortly discovered that her bum was especially sensitive. She pulled the girl closer, so massaging her lips as her tongue transferred into Eliza's pussy.

When it pressed, the priestess's body tensed and allowing out a shrill shout. Eliza brought a hand to her mouth to snack, while her other hand uttered Nalia's hair, pulling it off.

The concept was unmistakable. More, Eliza was yelling outside. Nalia's tongue tasted Eliza's sweet buds, rubbing back and forth because it slowly worked its way in Eliza's pussy. Each time that her tongue moved across Eliza's sheath, the bad woman shuddered. Eliza's legs were trembling in expectation and want.

Swiftly, Nalia proceeded to complete her hands reached up over her head, catching Eliza's breasts. Her thumbs discovered the woman's nipples and her hands massaged the flesh. Eliza couldn't result in the dual attack on her breasts and cunt.

Distributing a very long suppressed moan of perspiration, her entire body gave way. She fell on into Nalia, convulsions wracking throughout her entire body. It had been over a moment before her thighs introduced Nalia's head.

"This was... amazing."

Eliza gushed. Nalia nodded knowingly, even though her cunt was more than ever before. Make her do the exact same for you a voice. However, Nalia understood better. The priestess was hers for today, and she shouldn't squander it. Nalia climbed to her feet, however encouraging the tender priestess.

"This was only to block the spread of bad. There's a different ritual. Known simply to the Red Witches. Even stronger. Strong enough to purify you."

Eliza desired it. "Yes yes, we have to try this ritual."

Nalia shook her head sadly.

"It takes my abilities. Plus, then they..." she ran a finger on her collar.

"Subsequently, the collar has to go!"

The woman announced with sudden ferocity. She removed it using a bit as if it hadn't been procured on whatsoever. Nalia was liberated. She could sense her electricity returning into her palms.

She may have the ability to escape today.

Kill the woman, save Raum, ruin this location, a voice within her whispered. However, Nalia's eyes lingered on Eliza; she can see the want in the woman's figure, the expectation in her eyes, that the sweat between her breasts. Nalia set a hand beneath her skirt. Her pussy was a furnace. Her underclothes were also saturated. Something touched Nalia's heart, or maybe a little lower.

"On your knees, woman. Hands-on the floor."

Eliza obeyed. Nalia pushed her down the vulnerable back, forcing her torso to the ground and lifting her buttocks into the atmosphere.

"Where does bliss live?"

"In... in my bum," Eliza handled. Nalia slapped. Eliza screamed.

"And you've got as much excitement."

Nalia pushed her finger from Eliza's next opening.

"No more... no, please. Anywhere but there."

"But this really is where your bliss is, do not you would like to get purified?"

Nalia probed, analyzing her immunity.

"I... I..." The woman stammered. Nalia's other hand found Eliza's pussy; it had been even wetter than previously. Stroking her hands gently within the priestess's clit, then Nalia murmured to her ear,

"And if the mouth can lie, then your system doesn't."

Eliza could just moan, arcing her entire body and pressing her delicate breasts at the floor.

Her bum wavered uncertainly from the air for a minute. Nalia pushed her edge; her finger slid into Eliza's buttocks.

"There." She murmured as Eliza groaned. However, if her mouth is silent, her entire body has been ecstatic. Her hips moved against Nalia's hand, pressing demanding.

Nalia ran down her tongue Eliza's spine, savouring the strain in her muscles, and pushed her hands only a little further in. Eliza broke. With a shout, she pulled her legs together, bucking frantically from the atmosphere because her muscles convulsed.

Nalia attracted another finger in her ass, as her hips rose and dropped desperately fucking Nalia's palms.

"Fuck me!"

The woman cried in delirium. As suddenly as she began, Eliza failed. Her bum dropped to the floor and that she lay motionless. Tears stained her eyes again.

"Eliza?" Nalia asked tenderly.

"Oh it is all destroyed is not it?"

"It is?"

"I have not been purified in any way; I only desire. It was my secret, you understand. Whenever anybody brushed against my bum, I turned out, well, you understand."

"Horny as a bitch in heat?"

Nalia helpfully provided. Eliza blushed.

"Yes. And how do I go back today?

I would like to feel like this again. I would like to feel like this daily. Are you very wicked?" Nalia smiled, stroking her hair.

"You're. So really, very evil. Come together, and I'll show you joys beyond your wildest fantasies." Her eyes opened wide.

"Together with you? You are escaping?"

Nalia nodded.

"Together with my abilities back, if you will show me Raum's room, then we could be in our way" Eliza shook her head. Her hands are reaching under Nalia's skirt.

"Maybe not yet. Not while you are... well... I believe it just would not be appropriate."

Nalia supposed to the thing, supposed to inform her escape was important anything her body desired, but her mouth had been coated in Eliza's delicate lips.

The priestess's tongue pushed its way into Nalia's mouth and then ripped her breath away. Her hands pulled Nalia's skirt because her breasts pushed against Nalia's torso. Nalia hadn't been so near another girl. Eliza was burning as if she would catch on fire at any time.

Her tongue suckled Nalia's nipples, then educated her earlobes, and followed a route between her breasts and down into her belly. Nalia was in this type of enjoyment that she almost did not hear the click of their collar.

"Wha-!"

She tried to inquire, but rather she sensed passion seeping through her entire body.

"I understand your secret also. I am aware that you enjoy the pain."

No, Nalia needed to shout, but she could not locate the voice. Her thoughts might deny joy; however, her body couldn't.

Nalia dropped to her legs around the floor, cunt waving in the atmosphere, at precisely the exact same position Eliza was a minute ago.

Eliza's mouth discovered Nalia's womanhood; her hands found her clit. Alternating waves of pain and pleasure rocked Nalia's entire body, each one building on the opposite. Eliza's tongue had been within her, sparking her sheath in a sense she hadn't ever imagined.

Nalia's buttocks moved to fulfil her tongue. Deeper, she believed, as her hips rocked back and forth. Eliza twisted her clit, and Nalia nearly passed out in the double waves of pain and pleasure which washed through her.

Sharp nails bit into her hands, scraping her flanks because her body came back over and over on Eliza's waiting, hungry tongue. Nalia's body cried in her orgasm, not able to include the joy that she let out a shout.

Her orgasm washed through her and touching her shoulders, her nipples her cunt her thighs. Every part sensed that the discharge felt that the double agony and bliss. Another orgasm followed on the heels of this very first before Nalia fell in exhaustion.

"no time for this," Eliza said, giving her a hand,

"We must escape."

I am Robbing You

Elena felt something lightly touch her anus, and she awakened from sleep at the shadow. It was a hand, a hot hand. She murmured and nuzzled it caressed her lips and throat.

She had been dreaming. Was she dreaming? She had been lying in her large comfortable bed.

Alone.

Alone since her husband was away on a business trip.

She began, rousing herself out of the fuzziness of sleep and noticed a guy was standing in her bedroom. She turned on the light next to the mattress, and the stranger said,

"Good night, Elena, sorry to disturb you."

She shrieked and clutched the covers about himself, an intuitive but futile gesture. The guy smiled down at her.

He had been young -- at his mid-twenties -- also had pubic hair and green eyes. He wore a black hoody on a black t-shirt.

"Who the fuck are you? Get the fuck out of this" She cried.

He held his hands on his lips.

"Shhhhh," he explained.

"Do not shout, ok? I mean, there is no chance anyone's going to listen to you, about here, but..." he said, placing his hands into his pocket. Is he own a gun? A knife? She started hyperventilating with terror, her eyes filling with tears.

"Shhhh,"

he explained.

"Shhhh, calm down. Just calm down again.

I am only a thief—a burglar.

I am here in order to rob you. That is all.

I am not going to hurt you anymore. Okay?" She nodded her head, her breath whistling raggedly and immediately through her lips.

"Alright? Say that you know I am not likely to hurt you."

"I know that you are not likely to hurt me," she explained quickly.

However, did she think it? He surely did not seem barbarous, but the information was filled with images of guys who did not seem vicious.

"How do you get in here?"

"Shit, the kitchen door was not even locked."

"I suggest, beyond the gate?"

"These gated communities really are incredibly simple to enter. And if you are young and white, then it is unlikely anyone will also ask you a question. Those rent-a-cops are likely sleeping anyhow."

"What do you really desire?"

She asked.

"I am robbing you," I told you.

I didn't understand you're here. I knew that the husband was off on a business trip, and I believed you went."

"I was not feeling well," she explained.

"I simply have to tie you up, after which I'm likely to take a few things, and I will leave."

"Tie me up" She explained in a little voice and pulled the covers across her.

"Yeah," he explained.

"I am going to tie you up, and therefore you don't phone anyone and form through a few things, and then I will be gone."

She looked around; would she make a rush for it? Can she make it on your telephone, and from this space?

"Do not attempt it" he stated, again, but with a chilly assurance that indicated she would not have a lot of possibility of escaping if she conducted.

"How are you really going to tie me up?" She asked timidly.

"To the mattress articles," he explained.

"Only there; it is possible to lay there while I look up. Return to sleep."

"However... I Will... how long can be tied up?"

"Look, unwind. Before I depart, I will untie among your arms. From the moment you untie yourself, I will be gone." She looked at her enormous blue eyes wide.

"Can you guarantee that you won't harm me anymore?" She explained in a little voice. "Obviously," he said.

"I promised I would not hurt you."

He pulled away from a coil of black rope out of his jacket pocket.

"Nylon Paracord. Connect the end into a left ankle."

She looked fearfully at it, even flinching as if he had pitched a snake about the mattress.

"Come," he said, placing his hands in his jacket pocket.

"Can it," he explained, a bit more firmly. "Alright!" She said hastily.

"I shall... however, I, I am just wearing my nightie... may I, will I get dressed?" She asked.

He caught the covers and pulled them off her, then throwing the thick duvet on the ground. She shrieked back and pulled up her legs and caught them instinctively bending into a ball. She was wearing just a brief, mint green spaghetti-strap camisole and a pair of white cotton underwear.

"Look," he explained.

"I have seen lots of images of you in panties and bikinis in publications and online. I would like to get out of this fast, ok? Thus, let us get going.

Connect that cable around your ankle." He had been talking more crisply and ardently today, glancing down at her.

"Alright! All right!"

She explained.

"Alright, I will do it, only... okay, continue."

She tickles the green string; her hands were trembling. There were approximately 5 feet of this. She wrapped an end of it about her slender light shoulder.

"Wrap it about two, then tie a knot."

"I really don't... I really don't understand how," she moans, and felt tears rolling down her face.

"You are doing fine," he explained.

"I am certain you tie your shoes sometimes," he said mockingly. She tied a knot in the string, and then he moved forward and caught the other end of it, and pulled it tight and wrapped the other end around the bedpost.

"Nooo,"

she moans, beginning to sniffle and cry.

"I really don't wish to get tied up," she said because her leg extended out directly towards the bedpost. "Alright, now another arm," he explained. He pitched another little spiral of paracord back on the mattress.

"No," she said petulantly.

"One foot is sufficient!"

"Allow me to show you exactly what I found,"

he stated and removed his hands out of his pocket. Inside was a black plastic square; she realized: her stun weapon. She had always carried it in her handbag; the two electrodes could administer 50,000 volts, that could instantly incapacitate anyone unlucky enough to get them. She tickles and wrapped the next amount of paracord around her buttocks.

He immediately caught the other end and stretched into another bedpost, pulling down her legs. She automatically cried as her thighs spread, covering her crotch with her hands and attempting to pull back her leg but he pulled the paracord tight and tied it securely to another bedpost.

"Shhh," he explained. "It will be fine. Practically there."

He flexed and assessed the knots.

"Doesn't harm? Tight?" He assessed out the knots and appeared happy with them.

"It does not hurt," she sniffled. Not yet, anyhow.

"I... only, fine, only get your things and go, ok?"

"I have not tied your hands" he explained."

No, do not tie my hands-free!

Please! Look, I am tied up! I cannot escape from those knots with no hour of choosing them with my fingernails! And that I can hardly reach them" she pleaded.

He did not respond, only grabbed her wrist and wrapped a loop of paracord about it. She cried again and began to attempt and twist with his grip, and now he struck a hand on her mouth.

"Look," he stated. "I told you to not shout."

He had been sitting on the mattress today, over her, then imposing, his hands digging into the trunk of the face. "Only allow me to tie you up, and this will be finished. I stated I would not hurt you.

Therefore, don't make me do this, alright?"

He had been looking down at her today with no of this fantastic humour she had noticed in his eyes earlier. She nodded her head and left an optimistic noise, muffled by his own hands. Her blond hair has been falling from her eyes today.

His grasp was firm but instead tender -- he had powerful fingers, but they were very tender -- and then wrapped her wrist using all the paracord, then tied into the headboard of this bed. He tied her right wrist did exactly the same, and she had been tied spread-eagled about the mattress.

She began crying again, feeling totally helpless. With no duvet that the air conditioning appeared too large; it was cold in the area. She was conscious her nipples were so hard, and her skin had been buzzing with gooseflesh.

It was not the first time she had ever felt vulnerable and helpless, but it had been the very first time in several decades.

"There," he said, and stepped back and looked at her, he was grinning again. "Okay. Moving to go do some work today. I will be back to check you soon."

Ten minutes after, he fled to the area. She had attempted to escape out of the cable; however, the more she fought, the longer it appeared to bite into her flesh, and also on her back together with her wrists spread, she appeared to lack the grip to pull firmly in almost any way.

She put in the dark crying and thinking for some time, shuddering with dread. He was currently carrying just two of the husband's pricey suitcases. One of these appeared to be complete; she presumed it was currently filled with a number of her husband's most pricey things.

"Thus," he explained.

"Now the toughest part for you. I will steal some of the things."

She left a whimpering sound.

"Are you ok? Do you need anything to drink?"

He asked. He seemed honestly worried. Such a fine, adorable, innocent-looking man. She believed it.

"No," she stated. She did not understand how long she would be here and did not need to should use the restroom.

"However, please, how do you need to steal my items? My spouse has lots of things here that you take, really precious matters!" He looked at her thoughtfully.

"Oh, the poor little rich girl does not need to lose her items? Your husband will get you more, will not he" She began to talk, then stopped.

"Oh?" said the stranger, looking at her, amused.

"He will not get you more things?"

She looked out, turning her head with her arm.

"Hmmm," said the stranger."

"Some sort of trouble in heaven? The life span of a prize wife not all it's cracked up to be?

Your fat wealthy husband ends up to be a stingy bastard, after all."

She shut her eyes and stated,

"The financial crisis affected all people."

"Hmf," he said, starting her walk-in cupboard, and looking seriously at all of the pricey designer clothing and sneakers.

"Yeah, I could see that. This cupboard is larger than some apartments I have lived in."

"So that gives you the right to tie up people and steal their things?"

She explained, finding a few angers burning underneath the helpless exposure she believed. "Hmm, no, obviously it does not," he said absently.

"No proper about it. Much like you do not possess any right to all of this stuff. You simply took it?"

"They had been gifts!" She explained.

"Well, easy come, easy go," he said softly. He eliminated a few handfuls of clothing and tossed them onto the ground.

"You are aware that it is not the very first time that I've been here," he explained. "I have been here before."

She looked at him. She believed she'd detected several things lost lately -- some jewellery, some clothing -- she had a lot of things; it was really difficult to keep tabs on everything. She had assumed her mum or seeing friends had uttered the items.

He opened the jar which contained all of her panties, and she stated, "Hey! No!" He came back to the bed, taking out a large double few of her panties.

"Are you kidding? Here is the very best part."

She looked at him, eyes wide with dread, as he fell the panties on the mattress and started sorting through it.

He picked a couple of underwear -- he appeared to favour the light colours -- and chucked them at the pile of clothing he was amassing. Then he picked a couple of figurines and pulled at the developing heap.

She bit her lips again. What exactly was he planning to do with these? Somehow she did not believe he was planning to offer them on eBay.

"Obviously, I have seen you in panties many occasions in magazines and things, but it's a true treat to see you live and in person," he stated, now starting to form through her jewellery.

"I do not have makeup," she said absently.

"Do not worry; I still would rather the natural look" He lifted something.

"Wow!" He explained.

"There is a great deal of fine jewellery; however, this really is something exceptional." He had been examining her favourite -- a necklace using an emerald necklace which was worth over her Mercedes.

"No!" She cried.

"Do not take that."

"Fatass will get you a brand new person," he explained. "No, look... fine, but he is... we are likely to be getting a divorce shortly. "

"Is not this thing "

He asked. "I... I really don't understand. Please, take each of the other things, but make that."

"Awww, poor baby,"

he explained. He sat on the edge of their bed.

"Well, what can I buy if I abandon it?"

He asked. She looked fearfully at him.

"Exactly what do you believe? What do you desire? Would you like cash? There is $50,000 money in the safe in his office."

"Yeah, I understand," he explained.

"That was, anyhow. I took it. I mean, exactly what are you really going to provide me with that is yours, even if I abandon this particular necklace?"

"I... I do not understand..." she said gently and looked away.

"What do you really desire?" "Hmm," he explained.

"What would I need. Well, seeing you tied up on your nightie about the mattress, I have to acknowledge I really do get a few, uh, sensual urges."

She sobbed and looked off and started crying.

"That is really a nightmare," she sniffled. "Hey! Shhhh, shhh, it is fine," he said, and touched her anus; she flinched from his touch, then relaxed, and she stroked her cheek gently. "I am not likely to get anything, I told you.

I am not going to hurt you anymore. I told you I'm only here to give you."

He stood and chose the bead necklace.

"Anyhow, this item will look fantastic with this stripper I understand," he said and winked at her. "No!" She explained.

"Alright, please, now look what exactly do you need from me?"

"Hmm, well, I will leave that up to you. Make me a deal; perhaps I will rethink what I slip."

He stepped back to the cupboard and emerged a minute later carrying her white sable coat. "Hey, this is fine also. Obviously, it is way too hot around here to put on them, but there is a fantastic resale value on those, into these Russian gangsters."

She left a moan of bitterness. She adored that sable jacket.

"Yeah, you are Russian, are not you? You girls really like to use dead animals," he said disparagingly.

"I am homeless," she explained softly.

"If you understood exactly what it had been like there at which I dwelt, you would not believe it so odd that I like fine things. Or hot coats."

"So what, you climbed up on a plantation, needed to consume fresh veggies and things? Boohoo." "It was not like this!" She said harshly.

"It had been an industrial town, and there wasn't anything but contamination and migraines" He picked her up MacBook Air along with her iPhone in the nightstand and that she cried out as if he had struck her.

"Do not take these! Please! There is a good deal of stuff on there which cannot be replaced."

"Where? On the telephone or on the pc?"

He asked. "Both!" "Hmmm," he explained. He sat on the edge of their bed and opened up the telephone, appearing through it.

"Photographs of you and your idiotic buddies at nightclubs... dopey programs... some episodes of dopey fact show.

Kind of difficult to think none of this may be substituted," he explained.

"Aha! Below we are. A whole lot of nude images of you. What is the big deal? You believe that it'll destroy your career."

"No, it is only..." she whined. He appeared in her craftily.

"Ah-ha... who shot these images?" She looked out again. He started her pc; she began to protest then little her eyebrow.

"Some precious materials here, which cannot be substituted. Hmmm..."

She turned her head on the side and attempted to bury her face in her arm. He found it fast enough; she had only made it two times before.

"Aha! Well, Elena, you're a bad woman! A sex tape! Who's this muscle gentleman? He's ripped!" Said the thief, grinning at her.

"My personal trainer," she said.

"Well, that is not so original. Anyhow, it all becomes apparent. You are terrified that if I carry all of this stuff, these videos and pictures will soon be made public, and which is going to be the conclusion of whatever enormous divorce compensation you aspire to escape your fatass husband."

She simply made a whimpering sound. "What exactly are you really going to do to me, hmmm?"

He stated, looking honestly at her. She began crying.

"I really don't understand."

"I believe you understand," he explained.

"I believe we know how you generally get exactly what you would like." She awakens, more tears trickling down her face.

"All right," he explained. "We will begin with a reasonable trade. Let us see -- that the platinum necklace. I will exchange it to the camisole you are wearing today." Her breathing quickened as her heart leapt in her chest. She could not look at him nodded.

"Hmm? Tell me it is fine, Elena."

"It is alright," she explained in a little voice.

"What is it okay? Tell me," he explained.

"You may shoot my camisole if you allow me to maintain the platinum necklace,"

she moaned rebounds, tears slipping down her face. He smiled. "Good lady. Lift your mind a bit," he explained, and gently slid the necklace on her head and then settled it on her throat, carefully placing the emerald ring between her buttocks, and had been heaving as she tried to catch her breath. She felt as though she was about to hyperventilate again.

"Shhh," explained the stranger.

"Just calm down. It is going to be fine. I'm likely to take a knife today; please do not be frightened." She left a high-pitched whimpering sound since her eyes fixed to the brief glossy blade he flicked from his pocket.

"Are you really going to cut loose?" She inquired.

"No," he explained. "I will cut on the camisole straps to eliminate of it."

She left another jerking sound in her throat and then turned her head to the other side, attempting to spoil her head against her left arm, and was still stretched out into the headboard of this bed.

"Please do not harm me anymore," she wailed. "Listen, Elena; you are likely to hurt my feelings! I told you quite clearly that I am not likely to hurt you anymore. But we only made a bargain -- that the platinum necklace to your camisole. Would you wish to change your thoughts?"

He explained. "No," she moaned, pulling on out the word. "No, you do not wish to change your thoughts, or not, you do not need me to shoot your camisole?"

"No, I still don't wish to change my head," she sniffled.

"Say it again -- would you really need me to reduce on the camisole off you today?"

"Yes," she moaned.

"Yes?"

"Yes, I would like you to cut on the camisole me off today," she whimpered.

"I mean, I am sorry to reduce it," he stated because he lifted one slim strap and then put the knife blade under it.

"But it is my right? I will do whatever I want with this, right?"

"Yes," she said, sniffling back again. She was conscious her back was arched a little and her breasts had been thrust forward. He cut on the strap but did not pull on the thin lacy cloth off her breast nevertheless. Then he cut another strap and left the cloth lying on her breast.

"Are you prepared, Elena?" He asked softly.

"Yessssss," she groaned, starting to weep more challenging. He pulled both thin straps and exposed her buttocks; the pink nipples were stiff and tingling. The camisole was a bit of cloth around her waist today.

She also felt her breath rasping throughout her mouth today. Then he hammered sawed through the face of this camisole using his knife and then pulled it from underneath her, and chucked it upon the heap of clothing he was amassing. He had been admiring her breasts again.

"And they are real, also?"

"Yes," she whimpered.

"Please don't hurt me."

"Shhh, Elena, shhh, I am not likely to hurt you," he explained.

"Where did you get this notion? I am not likely to do anything that you do not need me to perform." His face was near hers now.

"Oh god," she moaned. "Oh my god, please allow me to proceed, please only leave."

"Ok," he explained.

"I will take the sable along with your telephone and the pc and proceed." He awakened. "Nice meeting you, Elena."

"Wait! No!" She said, screaming.

"Please don't."

"Listen," he explained. "I am getting tired of the. You simply continue crying, do not, do not. You tell me exactly what you do need me to perform "

"Do not make me!" She explained.

"Say what? There is nothing to say, however. I provided you with fair transaction, do you prefer to create another?"

"Yes!" She said urgently.

"And what exactly do you need to offer you?" He was smiling.

"Alright," she said, sniffling again, blinking her eyes again.

"My underwear. My underwear for your sable."

"Now, you are thinking!" He explained. "Good lady. And you also do not mind if I cut off?" "No," she explained tearfully.

"Simply cut them off, it is fine."

"Alright,"

he said, assessing her thighs and waist. He deftly cut the face of the waistband of her panties, also in a single simple motion had fully removed them. She was completely nude, shuddering, trembling, gasping and writhing from her bonds, even spread-eagled about the mattress.

"How do you feel today, Elena?"

He asked, grinning down at her.

"Oh god," she moaned.

"Helpless. Vulnerable."

"Excited?"

She left a whimpering sound again and attempted again to conceal her head off her arm.

"I should acknowledge,

"he said, moving his head near hers again, talking softly to her ear.

"I sort of did understand you were here."

"You did?" She inquired, her voice soft without dread.

"Yes, I did. And another thing on a few of those other events I had been, I stole your E-book reader."

She had wondered what had happened to this thing.

"And obviously I watched that the sort of things that you see, and I figure that way I understand what your dreams are, also,"

he stated, and she whimpered again.

"If I put my hands between your thighs, "he stated, now breathing in her ear," could it be moist down there today? I believe that turns you on more than it turns me on."

"Yes," she confessed, weakly, feeling the tears begin but feeling great aid.

"Alright then, I will provide you the telephone if I will touch down you and find out how wet you're."

She nodded instantly and stated "Uh-huh" breathlessly.

"Uh-huh, everything?"

"Give me the telephone, and you are able to touch me," she explained quickly.

"Sure," he said, moving his hands softly down her throat. Her thighs were straining against the bonds excitement; however, she relaxed a bit in the gentleness of his signature. His forefinger followed very softly on the glossy, swollen lips of her anus. She gasped with joy and pulled her head back against the cushion. He slipped his hands, teasingly up and down her moist slit.

She moaned and looked to his eyes again.

"Please," she explained.

"Put your finger in me."

"You are sure it will not hurt?"

He inquired taunting.

"I promised not to hurt you."

"It will not damage,"

she murmured,

"It will feel great; please set your finger into my pussy."

She had been almost whispering. She cried out in delight and pulled her head back once he added his finger softly into her moist anus, and then push her hips onto it then, maddeningly he pulled it.

"Wet down but not moist," he explained. He attracted the wet up finger and licked it, then held it in front of her head, and then she sucked it in her mouth, tasting her juices. His face had been hovering on her breast today, and she felt himself pushing him.

"Would you need me to lick your nipples, then Elena? They are so hard today; I suppose a wonderful sexy wet tongue will feel really wonderful. Your nipples are so tough; I figure they are very sensitive."

"Yes," she moaned. "They're. Very sensitive"

"Do you need me to bite it" "No," she murmured, "do not bite it. Please do not bite it."

"Just lick it? Kiss it"

"Yes... just be mild, lick it lightly, please, only lick on it lightly." His tongue swirled about her hard pink blouse, and she gasped and moaned.

"Can I touch it?" He asked.

"hello god naturally, yes, please, then touch with my tits, maintain them. I want to feel your palms," she moaned. His hands came up and covered her buttocks, as his mouth moved from nipple to nipple, kissing and licking, licking in the breasts while he pitched them luxuriating in her beautiful body.

She's gasping and moaning,

"Oh, oh, that feels really great, your tongue feels really good in my nipples."

His mouth was going down her belly today, blazing a moist warm course.

"Oh, yes, please, please," she stated, whimpering and panting, her body undulating contrary to his or her kisses.

"Please what?" He inquired, looking up at her, smiling. She strained her neck to check at him.

"Kiss my pussy," she whimpered.

"Kiss it, then suck on my clit..."

He pulled her pussy lips open with his hands and licked her clit softly, in precisely the exact same manner he had achieved her nipple. She bit her lips and attempted to stifle the rough yells appearing from her mouth again. He set her clit between his lips and started sucking and tonguing it gently at first but then more demanding. She cried out.

"Oh, place your finger into me," she moaned.

"Place your finger inside me." He slipped his hands in her as he continued to suck on her clit, and she bucked her hips and started gurgling and moaning in delight. She was thumping her head back and forth on the pillow, then babbling

"yes, please, please, please, please, please, PLEASE..." and he slipped two fingers to her and then curled them till he touched her gram.

She believed himself with an orgasm, then crying out hoarsely, her body spamming and bucking against the ropes which held her.

"Good girl, a fantastic woman," said the stranger, lifting his head from between her thighs.

"Kiss me."

she moaned, and her lips met, their tongues caressing, and that she awakens her wetness off his brow.

"Alright," he said, putting his trousers and eliminating his long thick penis.

"Today we will need to negotiate to your pc."

"Oh, god," she moaned, eyes still hoping to catch her breath.

"Please give it to me, I will suck on your cock, do not let me beg you to fuck my mouth..."

"Alright, open wide," he said, carrying her head in the hands and straddling her because he added his penis into her open mouth. She shaped her lips, creating a meaty noise of enjoyment and acquiescence.

She sucked it, moaning and murmuring her pleasure about it as he thrust in her face. Occasionally he pulled out, and then she chased it with her tongue swirling her moist pink tongue around the purple head and across the shaft as he caressed her face along with it.

"After all," he explained breathlessly, withdrawing.

"Would you like me to fuck you today, Elena?"

"Please," she stated, looking in his eyes again.

"Please fuck me, so do not tease me."

"Would you need me to untie you?"

"No," she moaned.

"I really like this, I'm being tied up and helpless such as that, I really adore being exposed..."

She had been conscious she had been babbling, but she had never felt like that before.

"All right, I will fuck you today..."

They cried out as he slipped his penis right into her glossy wet pussy. He encouraged himself with his arms so that he can look to her face whenever he pushes to her, slowly at first. She cries at her bonds.

"Please, please, more, quicker," she moaned.

"Are you sure?"

"YES!"

He started getting harder, diminishing himself to kiss her buttocks and throat while he did this. She screamed her joy in the ceiling. Shortly they're both gasping for breath, trembling, both the heat and pressure construction.

"Where would you really want me to cum," he said, ".

"In your tits, or in your face?"

"Oh, in my face!" She stated, hungrily.

"I need it all on my face!"

"All right, I'll cum in your head,"

he grunted, pulling and pushing his cock to her face as he spreads it. She extended her tongue, and once the tip of her tongue touched the tip of her penis, a hot squirt of semen burst into her face, covering her lips and forehead and forehead. "hello," she cried in delight, loving the sexy tacky feel of this. He fell on the bed alongside her, gasping for breath.

However, he immediately got to his toes. "This was fantastic, Elena; however, I have to run," he explained.

"Would you need me to wash off you?"

"No," she stated, shamefully, tired, shutting her eyes, feeling tears return, setting that the semen was drying to scales in her face.

"Can you untie me, however?" She asked in a little voice.

He pulled his knife and cut through the paracord holding her wrist.

"As I promised," he explained. He also covered her naked body with all the sable and that she murmured her thanks. He had been collecting the valuables.

"Alright, I will leave the pc here about the dresser," he explained.

"Once I make a backup," he stated, and added into a flash memory stick to the computer, immediately copying the movie for it. She had been so tired it took her a minute to understand exactly what he had been doing.

"What? No! You promised!"

"I promised I would leave the pc, and that I will.

But I'll continue to keep a copy of the video" He ended quickly and pulled on the memory stick out and then stuck it into his pocket.

Since he turned to depart the bedroom carrying the two totes, he looked back at her.

"We can pay attention to the yield of the movie sometime after."

"Oh my god," she said, horrified, unable to free her arm knowing she would never find loose from time.